GROWING POSITIVE

IN A NEGATIVE WORLD

Your Latter days shall be greater than yours former days.

Man shall not live by bread alone but by every Word that proceeded out of the mouth of GOD

Luke 4:24

GROWING POSITIVE

IN A NEGATIVE WORLD

JACK HOLT

ACW Press
Eugene, Oregon 97405

Growing Positive in a Negative World

Cover Design by Alpha Advertising
Interior design by Pine Hill Graphics

Packaged by ACW Press
85334 Lorane Hwy
Eugene, Oregon 97405
www.acwpress.com

Library of Congress Cataloging-in-Publication Data
(Provided by Cassidy Cataloguing Services, Inc.)

Holt, Jack.

Growing positive in a negative world / Jack Holt. -- 1st ed. -- Eugene, Ore. : ACW Press, 2004.

p. ; cm.

ISBN: 1-932124-25-X

1. Faith. 2. Christian life. 3. Positivism. I. Title.

BV4637 .H65 2004

234/.23--dc22 0403

Printed in the United States of America.

Contents

Introduction. 7

1. Developing Positive Faith Expectations 9
2. Anger—The Major Culprit Behind Negativity 19
3. Getting a Handle on Anger 23
4. Negativity's Worst Case Scenario 29
5. Breaking the Back of Negativity. 37
6. Creating and Maintaining a Positive Attitude. 53
7. Adjusting Your Attitude 69
8. Possessing a Winner's Attitude. 87

About the Author 105

Introduction

You can become a positive person and develop a winner's attitude regardless of the negativity of the world around you. Your faith expectations and your thoughts can be positive.

You can develop the champion within you, change your world, and write your own destiny with the words of your mouth, for Proverbs 18:21 says, "*Death and life are in the power of* [your] *tongue...*" You can get up on the inside (in your inner man) from the challenges you are facing right now and walk in victory through the words of your mouth. Jesus confirms this in Mark 11:22-26:

> *Have faith in God. For assuredly, I say to you, whoever says to this mountain, "Be removed and be cast into the sea," and does not doubt in his heart, but believes that those things he says will be done, he will have whatever he says.*
>
> *Therefore I say to you, whatever things you ask when you pray, believe that you receive them, and you will have them.*
>
> *And whenever you stand praying, if you have anything against anyone, forgive him, that your Father in heaven may also forgive you your trespasses.*
>
> *But if you do not forgive, neither will your Father in heaven forgive your trespasses.*

As you align your words with God's Word, you will begin to think like Jesus thinks and speak like He speaks. You will move out of the valley of death, defeat, and despair to the mountaintop of God's abundance! Then, as you exercise your faith—believing and speaking what God says instead of what you see—you will go from one mountaintop to the next! Your "valley" days will come to an end!

In this book, *Growing Positive in a Negative World,* I share with you some of the "how-to's" that will liberate you from negativity and bring you into a fulfilling life as a champion for God!

Jack Holt

Chapter One

Developing Positive Faith Expectations

Are you the kind of Christian that goes to church and asks, "What's the least I have to do to be a Christian?"

Well, I have to tell you, God is looking for people with a different attitude. He longs for those who would say, "Lord, I want to be all that You want me to be." He is looking for the champion within you to rise to the surface.

I don't know how many times in ministry I've had people ask me, "Pastor, will I go to hell if I smoke?" They are looking for the minimum. Usually I say something like this: "No, but you will smell like you've been there!"

We can't just skim the Bible and say, "I'm going to obey the letter of it." *We obey it from our heart—through faith!* That is what drives the champion in us to the surface. This is the key to positive faith expectations in life. When Christians only obey the letter of the Word, they have a negative mind-set and say negative things like, "I'm just going to do the minimum." However, in order to develop a winner's attitude, you *must* be willing to do the maximum.

To grow positive in a negative world requires positive expectations concerning your faith. It requires that you believe and obey God's Word from your heart—not just from the letter of the Word.

In 2 Corinthians, chapter 3, Paul talks about Christians being living epistles of Christ—models that other people can follow, and as a result, take on some of the same winning attitudes and expectations.

To grow positive in a negative world requires positive expectations concerning your faith. It requires that you believe and obey God's Word from your heart—not just from the letter of the Word.

Let's look at verses 2-6 of 2 Corinthians 3 to see what Paul has to say about you and me, as epistles of Christ:

> *You are our epistle written in our hearts, known and read by all men; Clearly you are an epistle of Christ, ministered by us, written not with ink but by the Spirit of the living God, not on tablets of stone but on tablets of flesh, that is, of the heart. And we have such trust through Christ toward God.*
>
> *Not that we are sufficient of ourselves to think of anything as being from ourselves, but our sufficiency is from God,*
>
> *Who also made us sufficient as ministers of the new covenant, not of the letter but of the Spirit; for the letter kills, but the Spirit gives life.*

It seems to be our nature to look for the minimums instead of the maximums. It is imbedded int our weak flesh.

Some people have asked, "Pastor, how many times do I have to go to church to be saved?" Or, "Pastor, what's the very least I can give to stay in good with God?" They need to solidly get this concept: Obey Him from the heart and see what happens!

God wants us to obey His Word from our heart, and that will release faith in the heart: Faith in your giving, in your service, in your love toward your wife (or your husband) and your children...faith and love for your country. God will do all these things with your faith, and He will bless you when you obey Him from your heart.

Under Law or under Grace?

When a Christian begins to head toward the arena of legalism, and lives off the letter of the Word, he has fallen from grace. The Apostle Paul makes this clear in the book to the Galatians.

Now, this doesn't mean that you are an immoral person. It doesn't mean you are living in adultery or out stealing. It simply means that you have stopped *obeying God from your heart.* The apostle was also saying that when you place yourself under the law, you come under a curse.

A simple way to describe the curse of the law is that it is a lack of succeeding at what you do, or want to do. That's all it is. Some people work around the clock and never make enough money. It's a curse that keeps taking away what they have.

In some cases, no matter how hard some people try to make their marriage better, it never seems to get better. The best they can do is to *maintain.* That's a curse. But when you obey the Word from your heart, you will break through and become a person of grace. Through your faith, God will begin to bless you, and all of a sudden, things will start to change.

Let's look at the Word to see how it is communicated.

In Galatians, Paul differentiates between obeying the letter of the Word in legalism and obeying the Spirit of the Word from the heart: *"For as many as are of the works of the law are under the curse; for it is written, 'Cursed is everyone who does not continue in all things which are written in the book of the law, to do them'"* (Galatians 3:10).

Then, in Galatians 5:4, Paul states, *"You have become estranged from Christ, you who attempt to be justified by law; you have fallen from grace."*

Positive Faith and Prosperity

Occasionally I preach on stewardship and giving, and I can sense when people close their hearts. It's not unusual for them to miss church while this message is on my heart. If they know it is going to be a six-week series, they are gone most of the six weeks. They close their hearts and don't understand that's why they are negative toward this subject and Biblical concept. They have closed their hearts because they don't want to obey from their hearts.

People who don't want to understand this truth have closed their hearts to the gospel message of prosperity, yet God clearly teaches us in His Word that He wants us to prosper. Things get tough and they don't have enough money to pay their bills, and then this message taxes them even more. But they don't understand, *this is the answer to their financial problems.*

The Bible is clear that tithers and givers who operate from their hearts will receive a surplus.

The Bible teaches, "*The blessing of the Lord makes one rich, and He adds no sorrow with it*" (Proverbs 10:22). The Word says, "*He who sows bountifully will also reap bountifully*" (2 Corinthians 9:6). Third John 2 says, "*Beloved, I pray that you may prosper in all things and be in health, just as your soul prospers.*" We could go on and on with numerous scriptures that declare *it is God's will to prosper you.*

The Bible is clear that tithers and givers who operate from their hearts will receive a surplus.

Malachi said that God would pour out a blessing upon the tither and giver that is so great "*there will not be room enough to receive it*" (Malachi 3:10). In olden days that meant you had to build more barns, but in our day it means we will have more in our savings accounts, or more perhaps investments.

Positive Faith and Obedience

When God called my wife Joyce and me to attend Rhema Bible Training Center in Tulsa, we sold our house and used a majority of the money to finance this aspect of our training for ministry. When we got to Rhema, I really expected God to bless us. I knew that if God told me to do something and I obeyed, He would surely bless me.

The first sermon we heard after arriving for Bible school was based upon Mark 10:29,30:

> *Assuredly, I say to you, there is no one who has left house or brothers or sisters or father or mother or wife or children or lands, for My sake and the gospel's,*
>
> *Who shall not receive a hundredfold now in this time—houses and brothers and sisters and mothers and children and lands, with persecutions—and in the age to come, eternal life.*

I didn't like the "persecution" part! But since that time, God has blessed me. I obeyed Him and did what He told me to do. The same thing will happen to you in any area, whether it's stewardship, serving, or marriage and family, if you obey God from your heart, He will bless you. Also, you will step out of negativity.

If you want to be positive in every aspect of life, you must obey God's Word, because God works through faith in His Word. Then, He will do *"exceedingly abundantly above all that we ask or think, according to the power that works in us"* (Ephesians 3:20). When you obey God in your heart, He will prosper you.

Negative people easily become judgmental and critical. They can get on the flow that originated with the spiritual death that came into the world when Adam and Eve sinned. When they get into this flow and mind-set, they get so negative that they attract problems into their lives. It's almost like a self-fulfilling prophecy.

Have you ever prepared to leave for work on a Monday morning and a tire on your car was flat? You change the tire.

Then, you get on the freeway and somebody cuts you off. You say, "It's going to be one of those days!" From that point on it doesn't matter what you do—it messes up! You have "framed" your day with your own words.

Because you were in such a negative flow, you attracted mistakes, conflict, and problems.

On the other hand, someone else can have the same things happen, but his or her response is, *"This is the day the Lord has made; we will rejoice and be glad in it"* (Psalm 118:24). Suddenly, the problems become *an opportunity for success* in their life.

I remember hearing a true story about a man who had a flat tire on the freeway. A guy came by and saw him with the flat and pulled over to help him. The guy who had the flat tire was a very wealthy person. After finding out the name of the man who stopped to help him, he thanked him for his kindness by paying off his house. *"This is the day the Lord has made; we will rejoice and be glad in it."*

You have a choice either to get in a positive expectation or to allow the world to put you in a negative one. But the negative one will destroy your life. The positive will direct blessings your way.

Positive Faith in the Marriage Relationship

During our marriage, my wife has come to me many times and said, "Honey, I want to do this." and I have responded, "No! End of story! I'm the head of this house. I'm the king. That's it."

Then, after a few days, the Lord would convict me, and I would realize, "This really means a lot to her. If I love her as Christ loves the Church, I should do this for her." The moment I go to her and say, "Honey, let's go ahead and do it. I don't want to do it, but I am going to do it for you because I love you," I can see how it causes our marriage to grow.

On the other hand, as a wife, you can close up and say, "I don't have to listen to him," or you can take the situation to the Word and say, "Lord, how should I be submissive to my husband? How should I obey him? How should I respond to this?"

I have seen negative attitudes at work in marriage relationships. Joyce and I have been married for thirty years, and I do not have a negative attitude toward marriage. But I hear it from married couples.

When there is a negative attitude in a marriage, the couple has already closed their hearts to the Word. The wife may say, "I tried that before, but he didn't change." Or, the husband says, "I tried to do what she wanted me to do, but she didn't respond." They get into a negative expectation so when the teaching on marriage comes, they close up and say, "Oh, yes dear, I'm working on it." But they are not obeying God from their heart.

Then, I've heard the women say things like, "All he wants is sex, and I just give it to him twice a month. That's it." Then the guy comes to me and asks, "Pastor, what do you think?" I'm not going there, brother! But I can send you to the Word.

The Bible says that the husband is to love the wife as Christ loves the Church (Ephesians 5:25). Jesus gave His all for the Church. Some guys won't even give their wife permission to write a check without their okay. Some give their wife "mad money"—five dollars—and say, "Have a good time this week." Would Jesus do that to you?

You trust in riches and you have to have so much in the bank in order to feel secure. When you trust in Christ, all you have to do is *obey His will from your heart* and you are secure.

You may have a reason why you do that, but that's not an excuse. Many times it's simply because you love money.

You trust in riches and you have to have so much in the bank in order to feel secure. When you trust in Christ, all you have to do is *obey His will from your heart* and you are secure.

First Corinthians 7:1-5 tells us that when you are married, you are not to abstain from one another unless you are in agreement and it is in the context of prayer and fasting:

Now concerning the things of which you wrote to me: It is good for a man not to touch a woman.

Nevertheless, because of sexual immorality, let each man have his own wife, and let each woman have her own husband.

Let the husband render to his wife the affection due her, and likewise also the wife to her husband.

The wife does not have authority over her own body, but the husband does. And likewise the husband does not have authority over his own body, but the wife does.

Do not deprive one another except with consent for a time, that you may give yourselves to fasting and prayer; and come together again so that Satan does not tempt you because of your lack of self-control.

If you do what God's Word says, your marriage will flourish. If you don't, it won't.

Obeying from Your Heart

In these illustrations, I have been talking about obeying the Lord from your heart. What is your heart telling you to do? Perhaps your heart is telling you to volunteer in church, and you should do it. If your heart is telling you that you need to try out for the band, then try out for the band. If your heart is telling you to give to missions, then give to missions. If your heart is telling you to go on a mission trip, then go on a mission trip. Do whatever your heart is telling you to do, for the Holy Ghost abides in you if you are born of the Spirit. That will put you in a positive mode.

In other words, God can send you to the most negative place on the face of the earth, and if you are obeying His voice, it will become one of the most positive experiences in your life.

Positive faith creates a tremendous expectancy, and suddenly your latter days are better than your former ones. You will find yourself blessed abundantly rather than getting in a negative flow.

Results of Positive Faith

Isaiah 45:3 states, *"I will give you the treasures of darkness and hidden riches of secret places, that you may know that I, the Lord, who call you by your name, am the God of Israel."* Look at this! *"I will give you the treasures of darkness..."*

What are treasures of darkness? They are abundance and blessing that you see outside of the church...in the world. Given to people who don't know Christ.

"The treasures of darkness" speak of the abundance of blessings God wants to give the Church.

So have positive faith expectations—expect God's blessings in your life!

Let me show you the results of having positive faith expectations—staying out of a negative, critical, or judgmental attitude but positive about the Word.

You can preach the Word of prosperity to people who are closed, and they may respond, "I don't believe that, Pastor. I believe we are supposed to go through life on Grumble Alley, next to Barely-Get-Along Street." You preach the prosperity message to some Christians and they get huffy and upset. But, I didn't write it! It's there...in the Book!

Many Christians are locked into their negativity, yet we have a *faith potential* in God to follow Him in a positive way. So I really believe when we read the Word we must have positive faith expectancy, and resist the critical spirit. We've got to resist holding on to things that we shouldn't hold on to. We've got to resist walking in unforgiveness. We've got to resist keeping records of wrongs and walk in love so God can bless us.

One of my favorite verses is Proverbs 13:22: *"A good man leaves an inheritance to his children's children...."* An "inheritance" is not debt that the children have to pay off after Mom and Dad die. An inheritance is leftovers! After the house has been paid for, after everything has been settled up, and the funeral expenses have been taken care of, there is an inheritance to give to your children's children. I like that!

You won't step into that if you stay negative or if you stay closed in your heart. I claim that verse so my expectancy is out there, and when the opportunities come, I will know it. Opportunities will come to me to help me be in a position so when I leave this life, there will be an inheritance for my children and their children.

Growing positive faith in a negative world is based upon the Word. "*So then faith comes by hearing, and hearing by the word of God*" (Romans 10:17). Faith is the good news of the gospel. The good news is that we are not going to hell. The good news is that the grace of God has been provided for our sins. The good news is that we have been redeemed from the curse of the law and from spiritual death. That is the good news, and we must stay in positive faith to receive God's blessings and continue to grow positive in this negative world.

In the next chapter, we will look at perhaps the major cause of negativity, so we can get a handle on it and root it out of our lives.

Chapter Two

Anger— The Major Culprit Behind Negativity

As a new believer I once had a face-to-face encounter with the anger that lurked in my sin nature. It almost overwhelmed me and I had one of those evil, fleshly moments!

My wife and I had a disagreement in the middle of the night and my flesh whispered back to me, "I'm just going to stay mad and teach her a lesson." As I look back on it I see how easily I could have avoided some real problems that ensued. I see how I had the choice to rebuke the thought and get over it, but I hung onto it. By doing so our relationship suffered the consequences. Even for the short while it lasted, it was not worth it.

The next day when I wanted to patch things up, I realized there was a problem I hadn't counted on. By putting off handling the angry moment and disagreement, I had created some negative results that were not easily made right. I had to do a lot of backpedaling (can you imagine me backpedaling? Well I had to do it to get things back on course.)

That's why Scripture says, "'*Be angry, and do not sin*': *do not let the sun go down on your wrath.*" Whatever it takes, it is vital to settle things quickly.

One of the major culprits that will bring you into negativity is *anger.* If you can master your anger you can master a good portion of the works of the flesh, and these works are described in Galatians 5:16-21. The works of the flesh are manifestations like jealousy, envy, and drunkenness. Interestingly enough, anger seems to always precede the works of the flesh.

As we desire to grow more positive in a negative world we must learn how to properly handle anger.

As we desire to grow more positive in a negative world we must learn how to properly handle anger.

By controlling your anger you can avoid such ugly manifestations as jealousy, envy, and strife. But when we continue to get angry at each other, at leadership, or at the government, there is no way that our world will be positive.

Ephesians 4:26-27 says, "'*Be angry, and do not sin*': *do not let the sun go down on your wrath, nor give place to the devil.*" Obviously, it's okay to get angry, but if you stay angry too long, it turns into bitterness. If it turns into bitterness, then you become critical and you get into a negative flow. Some people are still angry over things that happened months or even years ago.

Throwing Logs on the Fire of Anger

Initially, anger isn't necessarily evil, but if you insist on keeping it in your life for long, it's like a fire. You have to give it fuel and the fuel is this: If something happens on your job and you come home and complain to your husband, wife, children, or your best friends, you are adding fuel-logs to a fire of anger and it keeps burning.

As you go along with this unresolved anger you build a larger fire in your wake. The next day you start talking to people at work about it. You just add another log and the fire burns more and more. It then turns into bitterness, which turns into criticism and unwarranted judgment. It is not surprising to find yourself in a rut of a negative flow—which means you no longer expect good from God. You are expecting bad things to happen…and they will if you keep building the fire.

Here's how your fire spreads.

Your negative fire is burning good. The more negative you get, the more you keep throwing logs on it. You go over to another camper and say, "I want to tell you what happened to me. This is really bad. This person did this or that to me."

They say, "Hey, somebody did that to me too." Suddenly like a spreading plague they bring their logs and throw them on your fire. Now you have a huge bonfire. Immediately sparks fly and your wildfire glows red hot, and the whole forest ignites and proceeds to burn down!

Many churches are like that. They have been burned down by bitterness.

We are trying to save people and help them, but suppose an unsaved person comes to church desperately looking for God and sees our "bonfires" of anger glowing brightly. He sits on the row next to a person who has built a fire with his or her anger and he hears the bitter Christian critically responding to the preacher with, "Man, that's not true." Well, I can tell you the chances of that lost soul getting saved are pretty slim! I would expect that unsaved person to say, "I gotta get outta here. I can't believe these people. They are fighting with each other; even when I drove in here, the man driving the car in front of me was waving his hands and yelling at his wife, and the wife was crying. And to top it off, this driver turns out to be an usher!" If we are to win the lost, we can't be like that. We have to put the anger down. Just remember…it isn't a matter of who's right or

> Some things are just not worth fighting over. We need to pick our battles carefully, and resolve issues quickly. Remember…the world is watching.

wrong, it's a matter of doing God's will. To sum it up: Some things are just not worth fighting over. We need to pick our battles carefully, and resolve issues quickly. Remember...the world is watching.

You may have some logs of negativity that are still burning over something that happened years ago. When you are reminded of it you may throw another log on the fire. As long as you live that way, you will be judgmental and critical, but to walk down the positive path you must cease from anger. As long as you are judgmental and critical, your heart will be closed. As long as your heart is closed, you will not be open to the things that will set you free.

I want to be free. I want God's best in my life. I want His blessing to overflow abundantly in my life and in yours. It won't happen, however, if we are in a negative flow. Putting logs on the fire of your anger is a negative flow! We must be in a positive flow of expectancy with our faith, knowing that it is going to produce miracles and blessings in our lives. We must decide to walk in that.

I believe that when you feed on the Word, you naturally create a positive expectation. You will see that Jesus is a whole lot better than what someone said He was. Suddenly, like turning on a light, you now have hope where there was no hope before, and your heart becomes a channel for blessings to flow through.

In the next chapter, we will examine what Jesus said about anger and how to gain victory over it.

Chapter Three

Getting a Handle on Anger

"I just don't love him anymore."

I cannot begin to tell you how many times I have heard women say that about their husbands. It is a sad summary of relationships enshrouded with unresolved anger issues.

When I hear this I usually respond with, "Wait a minute! Hold it! There has to be something you liked about him to get married in the first place." And usually at that point we begin the process of rebuilding the relationship on a foundation of the positives rather than the negatives.

However, the problem that we need to look at is what caused these ill-feelings, or lack of feelings, in the first place.

Falling out of love with someone finds its core in having been angry with him or her for so long that love has no chance of surviving. However, it can be re-kindled if anger is dealt with head-on.

Harboring resentment toward one another, and acting out in anger, only adds miles and miles of cold distance between the two of you. When you are angry with someone and that anger stays in your spirit, it turns into bitterness, and the get-even sins usually follow. Whenever you are in that get-even mode, most of your decisions are designed to bring shame, inconvenience, or suffering to the person you are upset with. If you do that in a marriage long enough you will fall out of love with the one person you vowed to love all your life.

The truth of the matter is, Americans are selfish. We are not spiritual enough to fall back in love once we have fallen out. Most of us are like that, and we continue to shirk from long commitments, wanting things quickly instead. Living in an instant disposable society has been the breeding ground for this. Over the decades it has become the American way.

Here's the problem. If you fall out of love in your marriage, it is going to take watering and nurturing that little mustard seed of faith to get you back in the saddle. Many people struggle terribly in being caretakers of their faith. Soon they have no feeling at all and tend to lean on others for something solid. They find some other person who will agree with them, someone who will cosign their sin by feeling the same way they do. Once someone else endorses your sin, it (the sin) seems to become more and more justified and then off you go. It is a matter of guarding our hearts.

In Matthew 5, Jesus is talking about murder in a spiritual sense—not physically killing someone, but in the sense of anger.

In verse 22, He says, *"But I say to you that whoever is angry…"* The word "angry" here means long-lived anger. Not being angry for a moment, but someone who is carrying a grudge. So it is saying that whoever is angry or carries a grudge *"with his brother without a cause shall be in danger of the judgment…"* Jesus is talking about two forms of judgment.

Verse 22 goes on to teach us, *"And whoever says to his brother, 'Raca!' shall be in danger of the council…"* The word "council" in this verse is equivalent to our Supreme Court. In other words, if they were judged purely by the law they would be guilty in the Supreme Court and the penalty would be physical death.

Jesus is saying, *"Anyone who is angry to the degree that he or she says 'Raca,'"* is upset with the person. The tone of voice reveals that they are upset. On a purely justice basis, Jesus was saying, *"That level of sin is worthy of physical death."* Aren't you glad we have grace and mercy? Jesus is trying to show us the severity of this thing called anger.

Anytime anger stays in you, it is going to produce a negative attitude. A negative attitude is always going to cause you to be destructive toward those who are around you. You must keep a good perspective about people.

Everyone is under construction! No one is finished yet! So be merciful.

Everyone is under construction! No one is finished yet! So be merciful.

Now, notice the next part of verse 22: *"But whoever says, 'You fool!' shall be in danger of hell fire."* That's actually Gehenna, the lake of fire. In other words, the expression "you fool" casts doubt about someone's character (character assassination!). Jesus said if you were being judged purely on justice, you would be guilty enough to be sent to the lake of fire!

I avoid standing in the pulpit and slandering other preachers. I may preach the truth in opposition to what they are preaching, but I do not mention their names. Why? Because I am not going to be guilty of slandering them. So what is true in the pulpit is also true outside of the pulpit.

We should never communicate questionable doubt about someone's character into the minds of other people. All we can do is judge actions. Only God knows the heart. If someone is living with someone, obviously it's wrong, but I don't know the person's heart. I just know that the action is wrong.

Replacing Negative Thoughts with Positive Thoughts

Have you ever been angry at a person and after you go through the motions of forgiving them, you think you are over it, and then suddenly the thought comes back? I sure have.

There you are going along and someone reminds you of a past situation, and bingo…there it comes flooding back in with all the emotional reactions. It is at that moment that you need to say, "I am replacing that negative thought with a positive thought." Or, perhaps you need to stop and intentionally say something positive to counteract that negative thought you almost spoke out or acted on.

If we are going to grow positive in a negative world, we have to get a handle on anger.

If we are going to grow positive in a negative world, we have to get a handle on anger.

As I mentioned before, when a negative thought comes in about someone or some situation, stop and replace it with a positive thought. Don't just cast down the thought. Replace it with a positive thought!

You may be thinking, *I don't know anything positive about that person.* That's because you are still angry. There is always something positive about every person. Replace the thought. If it's your wife replace it with a thought of the qualities about her that you love. Obviously there are some qualities about her that caused you to marry her in the first place. Re-visit those qualities and thoughts.

In Matthew 5:23-24 Jesus said:

> *Therefore if you bring your gift to the altar, and there remember that your brother has something against you,*
>
> *Leave your gift there before the altar, and go your way. First be reconciled to your brother, and then come and offer your gift.*

In other words, your gift will not be accepted as long as you are upset with that person. This could be true with your spouse or with your children. "Oh, they make me so mad. I don't know how many times I have told them to be home on time." Or, "I've told her not to go out with that boy."

Suddenly you are bitter toward your children, and instead of speaking words of faith and life to them, you are speaking the words of death. Instead of using your faith to turn them around, your sin is setting them on a path of death simply because you won't change the way you think—which is usually justifying why you are right and they are wrong.

No parent would ever say, "I have unforgiveness toward my children." We can't because we love our children. But the truth is, there are many parents in the Christian community who live with absolute unforgiveness and bitterness because of disappointments and failed expectations in regards to their children.

Your faith will not work if you have unforgiveness toward anyone. So if you get upset, stay cool! Share how you feel, but don't exaggerate. Then, when that negative thought comes back, you can say, "No, I'm not going to think about that. I'm not going there."

In Matthew 5:44 Jesus said, *"Love your enemies, bless those who curse you, do good to those who hate you, and pray for those who spitefully use you and persecute you."*

If the challenge is in your family, speak positive words. It may take some practice but begin with saying, "They are positive people." "They are obedient children." You will surprise yourself how much peace and harmony will follow.

I feel very strong about growing positive in this negative world. Personally, I know that my faith does not grow strong when I am pessimistic about life. At times when I become negative I begin to believe in the things that I don't want—and that's exactly what I get. By speaking out like, "Well, I knew that was going to happen," or, "That's the way it always happens," you are only forming your destiny with your mouth! I encourage you to try using God's Holy Word to create the positive in your life and in the lives of those around you. Speak His truth and you will find the positives that you need to lean on and walk out.

Chapter Four

Negativity's Worst-Case Scenario!

Have you ever called someone on the phone and you knew they were home but they didn't answer the phone? You can imagine them walking over to look at the caller I.D. and saying, "Oh, that's just so-and-so. I'm busy right now. I'll call them later."

As frustrating as that may seem, many people are like that with God and the Church. God *is* calling. Whether it is through a manifestation of the Holy Spirit, a personal word from God's Scriptures, or through a manifestation of power, He is on the other line!

Our Lord longs to have a relationship with us. He calls and many turn cold shoulders as they check the caller I.D. and say, "Oh, it's just God. I don't have time right now. I know what He's going to say anyway, so I don't want to answer the call."

The phone calls are not answered and are continually put off until finally there is no way for God to reach the person. When that happens, He disconnects the line. Somewhere along the line that person accepted a negative perspective about Christ and Christianity, and the seeds are now producing fruit.

Let me show you one of the worst cases of what negativity can do to you. It is a serious step into a negative flow that effects eternity.

Hebrews 6:4 says this: *"For it is impossible for those who were once enlightened…"* (Because you have been blinded by sin you have to be enlightened in order to be saved. God has to open your eyes.) *"And have tasted the heavenly gift"* (This is in reference to eternal life and Jesus is the gift from heaven…and eternal life is knowing the Father and the Son, John 17:3). This all deals with relationship, and this person that the author of Hebrews is writing about has tasted of a relationship with God.

As we go on and read of more of Hebrews 6:4, it says, *"And have become partakers of the Holy Spirit."* This is more than being born again, because if you look in verse 2, it talks about "the doctrine of baptisms" (plural). When you are born again, you are baptized in water, which is symbolic of dying with Christ and being raised up with Him. The Scripture also speaks of "the baptism of the Holy Spirit" where the Holy Spirit fills you with power. So a partaker of the Holy Spirit is a born-again, Spirit-filled believer!

Hebrews 6:5-6 then says:

> *"And have tasted the good word of God and the powers of the age to come."* So these believers have experienced manifestations of God's power. As we read on it is summed up: *"If they fall away, to renew them again to repentance, since they crucify again for themselves the Son of God, and put Him to an open shame."*

This is a hard message. Verses 4-6 says that it is impossible for a born-again, Spirit-filled believer who falls away to be renewed again. How could anyone let this happen to him or her? They allow it because of the negativity they are condoning in their lives.

Negativity in the Church

How many times have we heard, "I don't go to church because it is full of hypocrites"? Or, "I don't go to church because years ago I did and the pastor ran off with the piano player"? People make sweeping, generalized statements like this out of excessive negativity. In their lives you can always find some reason they have become bitter, angry, and hostile.

Here's one that may not seem too negative, but it is, and I know you have heard it many times: "You don't need to go to church to be a Christian." Well, if you don't follow what God's Word says, you won't be in fellowship with the Body, and if you don't walk in fellowship with the Body, the blood of Jesus will not automatically cleanse you. If you're not automatically cleansed, you are defiled. If you are defiled, you are unrighteous. If you are unrighteous for long enough, you are going to open yourself up to demon spirits. If you go too long, you will become so hard-hearted that God will just shut you off. This is the worst-case scenario that can come from negativity.

Sometimes people leave churches because pastors offend them. (I don't understand because when I get offended I don't leave the church!) I can just hear it now, "That's the last sermon I'm preaching. They didn't buy enough tapes, so I'm not taking it anymore. They criticized me and that's it. I'm outta here, man. I'm not coming back." No, we don't do that…because it is answering negativity with negativity!

People make up a huge building project! They are always under construction, and some of them have postponed the construction. Many do so almost to the point that God wants to put an eviction sign on them because the construction process is so slow. I wonder if He sometimes doesn't want to say, "Come on, bring back the lumber and the carpenters. Your wood is rotten! Your foundation is rusting out."

These things will not happen if people get into a positive flow. When folks step into the negative flow, before long you can hear them saying, "I'm mad at God because He didn't heal Sister so-and-so."

We have to stay in a positive flow. We must fight to rid ourselves of this attitude in the church. I am so glad that when all is said and done, the Word will still stand true. Let God be true and every man a liar.

Believing by Faith

I'm going to show you what I have used over the years that has helped me bounce out of negativity and into a positive flow. It is all in the way I believe.

There are two ways to believe: You can believe by what you see; or you can believe by what you don't see.

There are two ways to believe: You can believe by what you see; or you can believe by what you don't see.

Thomas's faith is an example. He wouldn't believe Jesus was raised from the dead until he put his hands in His side and saw the palms of Jesus' hands. John 20:29 says, *"Thomas, because you have seen Me, you have believed. Blessed are those who have not seen and yet have believed."*

Are you ready to believe what God's Word says without seeing it in your life? This is how you bounce out of a negative situation, because in a negative situation, everything around you says, "This is what you are to believe."

"I'm not working."

"I'm not getting my raise."

"I'm not getting my retirement."

I have a good friend in his fifties who was laid off recently and is struggling to find work. Unfortunately, he had a number of years remaining to be eligible for retirement, which means he will receive no retirement income. At his age, and with the job market flooded with hundreds of others who have been laid off, finding another job is going to take God to do it. So he has a choice to make. He can succumb to the negative side and start the fast slide to misery. Or he can decide, "I'm going to be positive and believe what God's Word says. He says He will meet all of my needs according to His riches in glory by Christ Jesus. God's Word says a good man will leave an inheritance to his children's children. I am expecting that. I don't see it, but I believe it right now." If he chooses this path, he will move into positive faith.

Second Corinthians 1:20 says, "*For all the promises of God in Him are Yes, and in Him Amen, to the glory of God through us.*" Regardless of your situation, the Word of God is true. We must stay positive so God can do wonderful things in our lives.

Positive Faith for The Golden Years

I believe the older you get, the more you have a tendency to look at things and develop a belief system based upon what you see around you.

Most Americans believe that the older you get, the poorer you become. The older you get, the more sickly you become. The older you are the lonelier you are. That's not what the Word says, but that's what the average population believes. They believe it because that is what they have seen. The difference, however, is that we are faith people.

Psalm 103:5 says, "[God] *satisfies your mouth with good things, so that your youth is renewed like the eagle's.*" David wrote this psalm at an old age. He was accustomed to being blessed by God to the point of satisfaction. He then said in his old age that God renewed his strength like the eagle's. As eagles mature, they go through a molting process and all of their feathers fall out. Then they get a brand new wardrobe of feathers! In other words, David is saying, "I'm old, but God has renewed me."

Maybe you are young and this doesn't pertain to you right now, but eventually you are going to get a gray hair, or a few of them. Eventually you are going to find a wrinkle. At some point, your body is going to do some shifting. When that starts to happen, what you need to do is go to the Word. Find out that you

> You can choose to believe the Word, or you can just get old and wear out. You can age instead of just being happy and healthy as you get on in years.

are not going to become sicker the older you get. Yes that's true! The Bible says that God *"will take sickness away from the midst of you"* (Exodus 23:25).

You can choose to believe the Word, or you can just get old and wear out. You can age instead of just being happy and healthy as you get on in years.

There is a big difference between aging and getting old. Kenneth E. Hagin was a wonderful teacher and preacher of the Word of God. When he was in his mid eighties, he had more energy in his little finger than I have seen in some people who are twenty-five. For me...I'm going to believe God's Word that He will renew my strength. How about you?

Want to see something cool about getting old? Let's look at Psalm 92:13-14:

> *Those who are planted in the house of the Lord shall flourish in the courts of our God. They shall still bear fruit in old age; they shall be fresh and flourishing."*

The word "fresh" in that verse as used here means full of sap. That's positive. It is talking about a tree. In other words, you will be *vibrant with life* in your older years. The word "flourishing" means green and fat. So, the older a Christian gets, he or she won't become like a wilted plant, but will be strong!

I believe that when you follow God with all of your heart and all of your strength, He has special blessings for you. Look what the Bible says about Moses: *"Moses was one hundred and twenty years old when he died. His eyes were not dim nor his natural vigor diminished"* (Deuteronomy 34:7). Life is not over at thirty, forty, fifty, sixty, or even at seventy.

The Word has many examples and descriptions of having a vibrant life as we get older. Let's see what Joshua 14:10-12 has to say about vitality in your older years:

> *And now, behold, the Lord has kept me alive, as He said, these forty-five years, ever since the Lord spoke this word to Moses while Israel wandered in the wilderness; and now, here I am this day, eighty-five years old* [this is Caleb].
>
> *As yet I am as strong this day as on the day that Moses sent me; just as my strength was then, so now is my strength for war, both for going out and for coming in.* [In other words, "I am as strong at eighty-five as I was at forty-five!]
>
> *Now therefore, give me this mountain of which the Lord spoke in that day* [In other words, he's ready. He doesn't care if he is eighty-five. He wants to succeed and he wants to prosper. He wants the best of the land, and he is not going to back off because he is old. Instead, he's going for it!]

Some people get the idea that you have to be young to be blessed. To be blessed, all you have to do is have faith. Did you know that Harland Sanders started the Kentucky Fried Chicken franchise when he was retired? What a story of success! And how about the man who started the Lear Jet company? He was retired when he started this business. Bear in mind...it's not over until you are gone. God can use you for something wonderful in your life; all you have to do is stay positive!

Positive Praise Expectations

Psalm 34:1 says, "*I will bless the Lord at all times; His praise shall continually be in my mouth.*" Notice it doesn't say, "I will bless the Lord on my birthday." Or, "I will bless the Lord when I get my raise and my bonus." It didn't say, "I will bless the Lord when I retire." Or, "I will bless the Lord on our anniversary." No...it simply says, "*I will bless the Lord at all times...*" In the valley, in the hard places, and in the difficult places, I will bless the Lord.

Verse 10 of Psalm 34 says, *"The young lions lack and suffer hunger; but those who seek the Lord shall not lack any good thing."* "The young lions" is a reference to cubs or small lions that have not yet learned how to catch their own prey. It takes a year or two for these young felines to learn how to get their own game. During that process they are totally dependent upon their parents to feed them. But in the animal kingdom, the parent lions eat first. Then, if there is anything left, it goes to the kids. So as they grow up, they learn that when there is famine or pestilence, they are going to go without.

However, those who seek the Lord learn just the opposite. We find that those who seek the Lord in times of famine, God blesses. In times of drought, God comes through. As long as we keep that positive expectation of faith, God will come through and He will bless us. He will take us out of darkness and bring us into the light. He will help us regardless of what we are going through.

God will come through and He will bless us. He will take us out of darkness and bring us into the light. He will help us regardless of what we are going through.

Chapter Five

Breaking the Back of Negativity with the Right Faith

What if I told you that you have been given this incredible measure of faith? A faith that's not just ordinary? Well, you have it! You possess a unique faith that comes from God's Word. It is the Jesus-kind of faith.

I want to start with this very positive approach to helping you through your negativism. Why? Because when you are in a negative situation and the circumstances look bad, you need to know that you have this kind of faith to turn it around. If you don't activate and exercise this faith, it could be impossible to get the right perspective about it, and you might miss what God has for you.

Some people are naturally positive. They go to the doctor and he says, "You've got six months to live." The positive patient says, "At least I have six more months. I can get my affairs together." They can find something positive in it. However, I'm talking about something better than that. I'm talking about turning the testimony around. I'm talking about turning around what they were told at the doctor's office. Turning around what was said at the counseling center. Turning around what was said about their kids. Turning around what was said about you. That's what I'm talking about—a faith God put in every believer that when spoken, *without doubting*, can turn negative situations into positive ones.

There are miles of difference between a winner's perspective and a loser's perspective. If you can get a winner's perspective in any situation through God's Word, you will be able to grow in a positive way in a negative world.

What is the right kind of faith? Jesus describes it in Mark 11:23, "*For assuredly, I say to you, whoever says to this mountain, 'Be removed and be cast into the sea,' and does not doubt in his heart, but believes that those things he says will be done, he will have whatever he says.*"

There are miles of difference between a winner's perspective and a loser's perspective. If you can get a winner's perspective in any situation through God's Word, you will be able to grow in a positive way in a negative world.

A key to faith is having the right perspective concerning God's Word in the way that we look at things. When you have the right perspective, you can grow positive and your faith will grow. But when you are pessimistic, you will begin to believe in the things that you don't want. You will begin to believe that you will be laid off, that you are going to be sick, or that you may not have a long life. We want to go in the opposite direction—the positive faith direction!

Let's look at my favorite verses in the Bible from Mark 11:22-23. The setting is right after Jesus had cursed the fig tree. Twenty-four hours later, it had withered up from the roots. The disciples remembered that Jesus had spoken to this tree and saw what happened when he did. Jesus responded in verse 22. "*So Jesus answered and said to them, 'Have faith in God.'*" In the Greek, this means to keep having the faith of God.

Some people think that's a little strong, but a verse that confirms this is Galatians 2:20 where the Apostle Paul said, *"It is no longer I who live, but Christ lives in me; and the life which I now live in the flesh I live by faith in the Son of God, who loved me and gave Himself for me."* Paul is saying, "My life is absorbed in and controlled by the faith that Jesus Christ has given me."

Many people don't understand what it's like to have the Jesus-kind of faith. Faith comes by hearing and hearing by the word about Christ. So when you hear the Word, faith comes. But Jesus is the Word, so it's the Jesus-kind of faith. It's the kind of faith that God used to form history. Begin to confess: "I've got the Jesus-kind of faith."

Hebrews 11:3 tells us, *"By faith we understand that the worlds were framed by the word of God..."* "Worlds" as it is used here means generations. In other words, people who believed in God's Word framed generations. History was made. Moses and many others are classic examples of history-makers.

Anytime Jesus says "verily" or "assuredly" in the Bible, He is telling us something that has not been written in Scripture before. He is indicating that it is a brand-new revelation.

We see numerous examples of this in the Old Testament. Joshua, for instance, spoke to the sun and it stood still and did not go down for a whole day. It helped them to conquer their enemies. (See Joshua 10:1-14.) But the most clear illustrations and teaching on this are when Jesus arrives on the scene. He is saying, "All right, wake up! I'm going to give you a revelation, something you have never heard, something that has not been written in Scripture. I'm going to give you something that will give you fighting power against the devil." Then to make sure it goes outside of the camp of the apostles and into the camp of the whole Church, He says, "*Whoever* says to this mountain."

The mountain was the Mount of Olives, which is 2,676 feet tall. Can you imagine standing at the bottom of it while Jesus says, "If you have this kind of faith that I am talking about and you keep having it, you can speak to what you can't see over and

You *must* believe that you can change your world with your *words*. If you really believe that, when the world around you is producing negativity, you can speak forth from God's written Word and change it.

what you can't see through. In other words, the perspective right then is, this is impossible. But Jesus said, "No, this kind of faith that you have can remove the biggest obstacles, including the one that is right in front of you." A "mountain" was an graphic expression for a great obstacle.

I want you to get this in your spirit, because this is the key to becoming positive.

You *must* believe that you can change your world with your *words*. If you really believe that, when the world around you is producing negativity, you can speak forth from God's written Word and change it.

Producing Life or Death with Your Words

"*Death and life are in the power of the tongue, and those who love it will eat its fruit*" (Proverbs 18:21).

Have you ever noticed that when you are in a negative mood, your words are also negative. Well, negative words produce death, and I don't know about you, but I like life better than death!

My wife and I have a working relationship regarding our words. We tell one another when we are negative. A simple, "You are being negative again." works great for us. Joyce has a favorite expression when I am really overdoing it. She says that I am now being "Mr. Negatron."

Most of our problems would go away if we would learn how to stay positive in faith. Many of our problems are self-induced with the tongue. The Apostle James writes that your tongue affects the course of nature. It affects your moods and even your destiny. So if I am critical and speaking negative things that will send me on a course of death and destruction.

I'll give you an example. A single woman who has been burned in a relationship says, "I am nothing. I will never be anyone. If I get someone he will be a "flunky." If she stays negative like that, like a magnet of negativism, she will most likely attract someone who could abuse her and verbally take advantage of her. She does this attracting and is not even aware of it. Her negative attitude is causing it.

First of all, she has to deal with herself and begin to speak, "I am a somebody. I am a King's kid. I am not some beggar. I am a child of God."

Once she gets her identity straightened out and she starts thinking of herself the way she should, her chances of attracting a winner into her life are much better. I have been studying this for years and just now starting to get a revelation of it. It can turn a negative person around. Is there someone in your family you would like to be more positive? This kind of faith can change their life.

Your consistent confession can change the negative child into a positive one.

Knowing what I have just shared about framing and/or changing your world with your words, how can you turn things around?

Your consistent confession can change the negative child into a positive one.

At one time my daughter went through a phase where she thought she was ugly. She is actually really cute, but she went through this phase where she thought she was "ugly." So every time I saw her, I'd say, "You are so beautiful! I don't even want to stand next to you. I mean you are incredibly beautiful! You are a little princess!"

Of course she had started out by saying, "Dad, stop it!" However, within two weeks she was positive again about how she looked, and it was simply because I exercised my faith and spoke positive words.

What about a negative mate? What if a husband always brings up the dark side of everything you talk about? He always brings out the minuses, never the pluses. How do you change him? You won't change him by telling everybody, "My husband is Mr. Negatron!" Or, "If there is anyone who sees the black in a dark situation, it's my husband."

No, turn it around by saying, "My husband is a very positive individual. He sees the good in things." Then, when the wife talks to her husband, she says, "Honey, you're a champion. You're a winner. You have a perspective of seeing the good in everything." Go for it...call those things, which are not as though they are. At first, he may look at you like, "Woman, what's happened to you?" But don't let up...keep speaking those words which agree with God's Word and those that "frame" what should be.

You see...that's just a mountain. An obstacle that needs to be overcome. However, that word will begin to affect him and he will start to believe what you say, because it releases the force of faith and drives out the negativity that is in him.

I encourage you to start calling those things, which are not as though they were. (See Romans 4:17.)

How would you handle a wife who is negative? The husband says, "She is always nagging me. She is always on my case." Stop supporting the negativity that is working in her life. Go to your friends and say, "My wife is one of the most positive people I have ever met." Say it and believe it is!

I encourage you to start calling those things, which are not as though they were. (See Romans 4:17.)

Some people won't do this because they say, "That's not telling the truth." Stop right there! There are two types of truth: natural truth and Bible truth. Bible truth is more real than natural truth, because Bible truth comes from the Spirit realm. The Spirit realm is what created all things. You can go back to the Spirit realm and recreate things, even one's disposition, attitude, and aptitude. Go back and create these areas because there is power in your words.

When a parent is an encourager and speaks what should be over his or her children, these children frequently become high achievers.

When a parent is an encourager and speaks what should be over his or her children, these children frequently become high achievers.

This is not necessarily because there is anything special in that family; it is because the parents have the common sense and the wisdom to call those things which are not as though they already exist. They speak life into their children instead of death and they turn their world around because of it. Apply faith to the mountain of negativity and it will go!

Positive Winners in Marriage

In respect to this let's look, at Genesis 3:16 in terms of family. Adam and Eve had sinned. They died spiritually as a result of their sin and it affected their judgment and their winning perspective. In verse 16, God reveals to the woman the consequences of dying spiritually:

> *To the woman He said: "I will greatly multiply your sorrow and your conception; in pain you shall bring forth children; your desire shall be for your husband, and he shall rule over you.*

The word "desire" as used in this verse means to compel, to control, or subdue. In other words, the Lord has told the woman, "Because you are dead spiritually, you are going to have a desire to compel and control and subdue your husband. Likewise, he is going to have a desire to do the same, but in a way of ruling you." So God revealed the battle of the sexes.

Here's what I want you to see. These are two people who are dead spiritually. When you came to Christ, you became a new creature in Him. Now, you are spiritually alive. Your head is messed up, but in your inner man, you are not like that. When the mind is renewed to the Word, women will be treated in the right light, and conversely women will treat men in the same light. The end of continual friction will dissipate.

Have you ever noticed men expressing negative attitudes toward what they see as women's weaknesses? From childhood we develop an attitude toward perceived weaknesses of the opposite sex. How many times have you been driving with your husband in your car, and suddenly some driver whips over and does something dangerous and stupid? The first thing your husband says is, "I'll bet you anything that's a woman driver."

It's the same thing with women about men. Say a wife walks into the bathroom and the toilet seat is up. She says, "I can't believe it! He can't put that toilet seat down!" It may be that your husband didn't do it. I mean…it's possible. Not likely, but possible! Women get with their girlfriends and they talk about the weaknesses of men. Remember these are confessions!

Men and women alike have attitudes. We can't grow positive in our marriages if we maintain negative attitudes toward one another. We can't grow close because it produces a lack of patience with one another.

Years ago, a man in our church would not drive to church with his wife. Without fail when he would go with his wife she would have last-minute things to do. It became more and more difficult for her to get in the car when he wanted her to be in the car. So he said, "Forget it. I'm taking my car, and you take your car." He would drive all the way to church by himself, and she would come by herself. Where did that come from? To an uninformed observer it would look like a chauvinist pig perspective.

I have been frustrated with my wife, waiting for her at times, and I hate waiting for anything or anybody. But I do know that my wife has more to do than I when getting ready. I can get ready quickly but my wife is not quite as speedy. If we anticipate and know this, then the frustration is much less.

Men, women are beautiful vessels and it just takes a little more time. It is worth the patience to wait and deal with my anger. If I do I can ride to church with my wife and have that time with her rather than allowing myself to say, "I'll see you when you get there."

Because of negative attitudes, a lot of couples learn how to live together without spending a lot of time with each other. Their relationship begins to lose meaning.

The woman may say, "I'm not going to deal with you, Honey. I can't handle you anymore. I'm going out with the ladies. I'll be back this weekend. I just can't handle your dirty socks and your football anymore. I can't handle your leaving the plates in the sink instead of putting them in the dishwasher. I'm just going to split with the girls for a while. See you later."

The husband does the same thing. "I can't handle you, woman. Your nylons are always hanging in the shower. I'm taking off for the weekend. I'm going to do something with the guys. See you later."

What we need to understand is, if you can see the differences between a man and a woman, you can have a positive perspective about each other. And you can have patience with someone who is wired differently than you are.

Have you ever noticed that when you go into a grocery store or mall with your wife, the guys have an objective: Go in, bag it, and leave. For a long time, we would walk in a store and I'd say, "Focus, Honey, focus."

A woman will agree to go in and purchase something with you, but when she goes into a store, all of a sudden everything within the area becomes part of the process. "I've got to check out what's happening here," because in her mind she is thinking of anniversaries, birthdays, and future events. Her mind has this entire scenario going on, but most men have a one-track mind.

Men and women are wired differently. If you do not understand this, it can cause conflict to the point where a husband will not even go shopping with his wife. It is really a shame to miss time with each other because you have no patience with each other. Shopping together can be an opportunity to spend time.

As men, we think, *Hey, we've got it together, man. We are productive. We are fruitful. We know how to get in, get things done, and get out. We're cool!*

But if you didn't have a wife, here is how your life would run. You would plan your vacation a week before or the day before the vacation is to start. Then you would find yourself at the mall buying socks and underwear—things that your wife would have bought four months earlier if you would have allowed her to do her thing when you went shopping together.

When you look at a woman like this, you will have a good perspective about her. She is wired differently. It may seem like a weakness, but actually it is a strength. The wife would look at the husband and say, "I know he is just results-oriented. He wants to fix everything that is broken. If I could just value that, what would it do for my marriage?"

You can be patient with each other instead of saying, "You do your own thing, woman. I'm going to do my own thing." That is the way the world behaves every day. Christians should be different than people of the world.

I have to have a positive perspective about my wife, and she has to have a positive perspective about me. Yet when ladies get together they sometimes have a tendency to talk about all the negative points their spouses have. And the same thing is true with guys. "Oh, yeah, he leaves the toilet seat up too?" "You wouldn't believe it! He won't put his socks away." "He drives me absolutely nutty. I've told him a thousand times to put his keys in the same place, but he always puts them in a different place."

We tend to laugh about these things, but at times it actually wrecks relationships. It's okay to understand and laugh about the differences, but when it causes you to not do things together, then it's time to wake up. It's time to say, "Listen, I've got to be patient with my wife. She is wired this way. It's a blessing."

It's the same way with your kids. Kids aren't adults. Some parents get all spaced out with their children. You have to understand, when you're a kid you don't have to pay rent. When you're a kid, the most important thing in your life is the cartoons on Saturday morning. That's okay, because that's where they are in life. It's neat to go through life with them and enjoy them as they are growing up.

We need to have a positive perspective and a winning attitude about our kids, our spouses, our church, and our pastor.

Believing the Bible is the Way to Success

One of the things that will cause you to grow positive in a negative world and break the back of negativity is to believe in the Bible promises of success.

For example, in Joshua 1:8 God told Joshua:

> *This Book of the Law shall not depart from your mouth, but you shall meditate in it day and night, that you may observe to do according to all that is written in it. For then you will make your way prosperous, and then you will have good success.*

When I study the Bible, I want to find out how I can win. I can win spiritually, financially, and in every area of my life. If I don't have that perspective concerning the Word, I will not be able to win in the area that I am struggling in. If I have a wrong perspective about prosperity, I won't be able to succeed in this area. If I have a wrong perspective about church, I won't be able to succeed in church. If I have a wrong perspective about government, I will not be able to succeed with influence in the school systems or in voting to bring forth a positive result.

Many Christians have a bad attitude about money in the church. You mention money and walls go up. You can't prosper God's way if you have a bad perspective about money. Why do people have a bad perspective about money in churches? Either they have believed a lie that is keeping them from doing the truth, or they have had a bad experience in relationship to money.

Here is a statement that may shock you. You can prosper and get rich without tithing. But it will not be with good success. The Bible says, "*The blessing of the Lord makes one rich, and He adds no sorrow with it*" (Proverbs 10:22). All you have to do is put money above your family, above your spiritual life, above your children, above everything in your life and go after it with all of your heart. Work twenty-four hours a day and you can become wealthy, but it will cost you your wife, your children, and your spiritual life.

Now, the blessing of the Lord is not like that. When God prospers you it doesn't cost you your marriage, your children, or your health, as long as you maintain a good perspective. You need to look at tithing and giving as an instrument of God to keep you from getting into the love of money. You need to look at it as an instrument for seeking first the Kingdom of God. You are putting God first so money doesn't get a handle on you and control you. Then the blessing of God will cause you to prosper without wrecking your relationship with your wife and your family or your spiritual life.

The prosperity of the Lord has safety factors in it. When you tithe and give the way the Lord says, and you become the steward that He wants you to be, there is safety.

Only about 20 percent of the people in an average church are tithing. Why is that? Because people are buying half-truths. You have Christians who say, "Tithing was under the law. We are not under the law. We are under grace." That's half-truth. The truth is that 450 years before tithing was instigated, tithing was implemented through Abraham, the father of our faith. We have a covenant with God and part of that covenant is that His children are tithers. Some people take a half-truth and miss out on true prosperity.

The prosperity of the Lord has safety factors in it. When you tithe and give the way the Lord says, and you become the steward that He wants you to be, there is safety.

Safety is this. God only prospers you to the measure that your soul prospers. "*Beloved, I pray that you may prosper in all things and be in health, just as your soul prospers*" (3 John 2). In other words, even as your mind is renewed to the point that you follow the leading of your spirit, God says, "I will prosper you." So God says, "You start tithing and giving from your heart, renew your mind with the Word, and as your soul prospers, I will prosper you. But if your soul is not prospering, I will stop right then because I am not going to allow that prosperity to take from you the things that are good for you."

If the financial area is a problem in your life, you might need a new perspective about it. If you are having marriage problems, maybe you need a new perspective. Maybe you need a new Bible perspective. If you are having trouble with your kids, most likely you need a better Bible perspective about them.

Get a winning perspective so that you can win. Before success comes good perspectives; and before prosperity comes correct stewardship.

Get a winning perspective so that you can win. Before success comes good perspectives; and before prosperity comes correct stewardship.

If you are growing more negative, you can go to church and have the preacher lay hands on you until your hair falls out, but nothing is going to change. Your soul has to prosper. Your mind has to be so persuaded by the Word that when the Lord leads, you follow.

This applies when you are in a store with your wife and she is taking her sweet time doing her thing and you are feeling more and more frustrated. The game is about to come on and you have been waiting all week for this game and you want to get home and watch it. Before you begin yelling at her, allow this teaching to roll through your spirit and renew your mind.

Think of those things that are good and pure. Think of the advantages of what your wife is doing for you. Suddenly, the Spirit of God says, "Why don't you just say, 'Honey, I'm going to sit down over here. You take as much time as you want.'" If you can, your soul will prosper.

On another note, and back to tithing...let's say you have been giving 20 percent of your income to the church. You feel pretty good about it. "I'm a big giver. I'm better than most people. Bless the Lord!" But you've been renewing your mind. Suddenly, the Holy Spirit speaks to you and says, "I want you to give 30 percent this year." You respond, "Thirty?"

You talk to your wife, but because your mind has been renewed, you test it to see if it is the Holy Spirit. After the Lord confirms it to you, you respond, "The Lord really wants us to do this," and your soul prospers.

Everyone can say, "I believe in it." But the leading of your spirit determines how much your soul has prospered. You need to renew your mind to a place that anything God asks you to do, you will do it—as long as you are sure it is God!

> You cannot resist the devil without the knowledge of God's Word.

Feeding Your Spirit with God's Word

In my own life there have been times when I became judgmental and critical, and it wasn't because I was angry with anyone. It was because of my *thought process.* I realized that the things you feed on will affect whether you are judgmental or critical. When you feed on the right things, they will make you positive. When you read and meditate on the wrong things, they will cause you to become critical and judgmental.

First Peter 5:8-9 contains another outrageously cool truth:

> *Be sober, be vigilant; because your adversary the devil walks about like a roaring lion, seeking whom he may devour. Resist him, steadfast in the faith.*

You cannot resist the devil without the knowledge of God's Word.

You need to study truth more than you study error. You need to study what God's Word says and not study the lies and falsehoods of evil.

There are some ministries in the Body of Christ that teach God's people about the occult and different religions. I want to give you a warning word of wisdom: *Don't study error to discern what error is. Study truth.*

An example of this relates to a bank teller. Bank tellers are trained to be able to detect counterfeit money. They are trained by studying real money so when the counterfeit shows up they can detect it automatically.

You can study the dark side of things so much that you become judgmental and critical. The truth is what sets you free. Error does not.

In First John, the Apostle John deals with Gnosticism, a perverted form of Christianity that was in the church at that time. As he begins to teach, he never mentions any of the error that these people taught. All he teaches is truth that would counteract the error.

The book of Revelation, when it talks about the seven churches, refers to wrong doctrine but it never tells you what the wrong doctrine is. Why? *Because the Bible centers on truth, not on error.* If you learn your Bible well enough, you'll be able to tell when something is wrong.

Some people are always attracted to the dark side or the negative. If you feed on teaching that majors on sin rather than on righteousness you will become critical and judgmental.

I have found that you will see lasting results with the study of truth. People change when they find out who they are in Christ. People change when they start acting the way they should in Christ. Lifestyle changes take place. It is most wonderful to see and experience.

Chapter Six

Creating and Maintaining a Positive Attitude

My wife loves shopping. I know that is probably not headline news since most women love to shop, but it will serve to illustrate how this affects my attitude.

During one Thanksgiving dinner I mentioned to my wife that I had Friday off and that perhaps we could do a little shopping. She slowly hung her head.

Surprised, I asked, “What’s the matter?” I thought she would be overjoyed that I had volunteered to spend some time with her doing her “thing.” Man, was I wrong!

“Honey,” she said, “that’s the most important shopping day of the year. I don’t want to hurt your feelings, but you are not a good shopper.”

I know this is off the chart, but it really caught me off guard. It was obvious that somewhere along the line I had displayed a negative attitude to shopping, and she had seen it. Even if it had been just a little bit of negativity, my wife is so sensitive to my attitude and she had picked up on it without mentioning it before. Now here it was—out on the table in front of me.

I sat and thought about it for a few minutes and realized that I did have some negative thoughts about this "biggest shopping day of the year." *First and most importantly,* I thought, *you have to be a professional shopper to survive the malls the Friday after Thanksgiving. If you aren't careful, spend-crazy women could stampede you!* So there it was…I obviously had projected this to her and my negative attitude about shopping was really showing. I had to do a reality check, and after realizing what was going on I knew I needed to know more about how to create and maintain a more positive attitude about even the seemingly little things in life.

I began with studying the word "attitude." Originally it comes from the word "aptitude." In other words, when you have a positive attitude your aptitude hits the ceiling. But if it is negative, it hits the basement real fast.

If we can create and maintain a positive attitude in our marriages, raising our children, our businesses, and in our ministries, then our faith will soar.

Getting a hold of this can give you an edge. After all, you have the potential and the ability to do everything God has called you to do! Capitalizing on this attitude business may just give you what it takes to go over the top!

Part of the problem we have is a lack of faith in God's Word. As a result, we lack a positive attitude in dealing with the problems we face.

If we can create and maintain a positive attitude in our marriages, raising our children, our businesses, and in our ministries, then our faith will soar.

It's really hard to maintain a positive attitude in life if you don't believe that your faith can change the situation. If you believe you are in a hopeless situation, it's hard to be positive.

Listen to what Jesus said to a man who questioned whether or not He was able to help him. In Mark 9:23 Jesus responds to him, "*If you can believe, all things are possible to him who believes.*" If I could paraphrase it, it would read something like this: "You have faith and if you choose to believe, all things are possible to you. But if you choose not to believe, nothing will be possible to you."

As I was meditating on this verse from Mark 9:23, the Lord shared with me that if you have enough faith to seek Him, you have enough faith to be delivered. In other words, if you have enough faith to seek after the Lord to help you with your situation, or if you have enough faith to seek Him for deliverance from whatever it is—financial, emotional, mental, or physical—you have enough faith!

Faith Speaks

The kind of faith that grows is the kind of faith that speaks. Jesus said, "*If you have faith as a mustard seed, you can say to this mulberry tree, 'Be pulled up by the roots and be planted in the sea,' and it would obey you*" (Luke 17:6). But *you* have to sow the mustard seed. When you speak out what you believe faith comes. The Bible is clear about it, "*So then faith comes by hearing, and hearing by the word of God*" (Romans 10:17). Many people say, "Faith comes as the pastor preaches." *But it comes when you speak out what you believe.* The more you hear what you believe, the stronger your faith will become and the more you will be able to overcome the mountain-sized obstacles and difficulties in your life. In other words, you can change your world if you change your words. Maybe you have been speaking negatively about your spouse, your children, your church, the government, etc.. What you need to do is turn that around and *start speaking positively—in faith!*

> Perhaps you are facing a situation that is so negative and your attitude is so bad you need to apply the Word and speak life into it.

Years ago when I did three services on a Sunday morning, I was so tired I would lie down for half an hour in the afternoon. I would have to speak to myself to get up: "I can do all things through Christ who strengthens me." I did this and am stronger today because I prevailed with His Word.

Perhaps you are facing a situation that is so negative and your attitude is so bad you need to apply the Word and speak life into it.

Start calling those things which are not as though they are, and start releasing God's power in your life. This positive affirmation could be something like, "My wife [or husband] listens to me, and she [or he] is so sensitive to me."

Here is the difference between belief and faith. Do you believe that Jesus Christ died for your sins and was raised on the third day? It doesn't do you any good to believe it until you confess it with your mouth. That's when your belief becomes faith. You have to confess it! With the mouth confession is made unto salvation.

It's one thing to believe the Bible, but it's another to *say* what you believe and *act* on what you believe. If we are negative, or if we have a bad attitude, we need to go to the Word asking, "Lord, show me in the Word the right perspective."

The Bible says, *"Let the redeemed of the Lord say so…"* (Psalm 107:2). Let me begin to say what I need to say in this negative situation so the mountain can be removed. At first your faith may be small, but if you keep saying what you believe and you keep hearing what you are saying, eventually your faith will be strong enough, and God will have enough access through that faith to remove the problem from your life.

Always expect God to be good to you beyond the goodness that you have already experienced.

Always expect God to be good to you beyond the goodness that you have already experienced.

> *I have been blessed but I always increase my expectations of God. When you have a negative situation in your life, you have to raise your level of expectancy. Expect God*

to do something more wonderful than He has done up to that point. That will bring you out of a negative spirit into a positive attitude. This will cause your ability in Christ to soar.

> No matter how good God has been to you in the past...keep increasing your expectations.

God has done more for us than just forgive our sins. He has provided us with His promises. He did more than rescue His people out of the slavery they were in for 450 years. He took them out of Egypt into a land that flowed with milk and honey. If you want to go into your land of milk and honey, increase your expectancy of good in your life.

No matter how good God has been to you in the past...keep increasing your expectations.

That is one of the keys to having a positive attitude—just believing in God's goodness and that He *is* going to come through. You can't bear too much fruit and you can't have too many blessings. Do you realize that every time you are blessed, God is glorified? There is no lid to how much God should be glorified in your life.

Putting Down the Works of the Flesh

Having dealt earlier with the issue of anger I will not beleaguer it, but one of the quickest ways to get a bad attitude is to have anger turn into sinful anger.

Ephesians 4:26-27 says, "'*Be angry, and do not sin*': *do not let the sun go down on your wrath, nor give place to the devil.*" This indicates that if you stay angry for too long, it always turns into bitterness, resentment, criticism, and an unforgiving spirit. We cannot afford to be angry for very long or it will turn on us.

My wife Joyce and I were blessed to be at a retreat in Oregon. I was sitting at the table with several pastors and their wives. As we were visiting, a friend who has a church near ours asked about our church. While I was sharing with him about our growth and how God was blessing us, a couple sitting next to my wife said aloud to each other, "Let's sit someplace else." By the tone, I assumed that they became resentful or jealous and didn't want to hear about the blessings the Lord has bestowed on our ministry. I was not bragging; I was only giving my friend an update and a praise report of God's faithfulness.

If you let anger stay in you, you will have a negative attitude toward the things that are necessary to correct your life.

Here's the problem with this type of negative attitude: Whenever anger turns into sin, you no longer have an ear to hear what you need to hear to go to the next spiritual level. Perhaps I could have given this man some advice that would put him over the top, but he didn't have an ear to hear. He had no idea that his negativity (jealousy) was making him dull of hearing and he could not receive from me.

Let me further illustrate how this works. Let's say Joyce and I just have an "okay" marriage. As many of you know we have a really great marriage, but let's say that it was just okay. Another couple is doing some teaching on family in the church and they mention that their marriage is stronger and is superior to ours. How do I react to this? Well, if I get jealous or resentful of them and what they have spoken, then I will not have an ear to hear what they say and likewise I will not hear what could help my marriage be even better.

If you let anger stay in you, you will have a negative attitude toward the things that are necessary to correct your life.

It's the same in a business. If you have been in a new business for only a few years, you may still be struggling or just barely making it. Then along comes a guy with a four-car garage, a swimming pool, and four hundred employees. Let's say this person wants to share some wisdom that could bring you more success. If you are negative with jealousy, you won't be able to receive it because you won't have an ear to hear.

As for putting things to death and overcoming through positive thoughts and attitudes, there are certain temptations that you want to avoid also. If you have a tendency to lust for women, then don't go down to the beach where they are not wearing much. If someone at your workplace doesn't dress appropriately, slap yourself in the head and say, "I put my flesh under." After all you cannot just stop going to work. You've got to provide for your family. You have to be proactive and tell yourself, "I am not going to look twice. I am not going to focus on this." You have to make a concerted effort to discipline yourself in these surroundings.

More on Jealousy

My wife Joyce and I have struggled with this jealousy thing for years because when we first started in ministry we were broke. I heard one preacher say, "You need three bank accounts," and I'm thinking, *Man, I don't even have enough to put in one.*

We would walk through the mall and look at things. I would grab Joyce and say, "Honey, this is crazy. We don't have any money. Why are we here?" Most of the time a disagreement would ensue and we would be at it all the way home. The frustration (stemming from jealousy too) was all about what we couldn't buy. After awhile I made a decision to approach it differently, and I decided that the times that I went to the mall with Joyce I would simply look and say, "One day we are going to have that, Babe. I can see that in our new house." I turned it around and allowed the positive to build the vision. The Word I used to arrive here was, "*No good thing will He [God] withhold from those who walk uprightly*" (Psalm 84:11).

Several years ago I was looking at a car to buy. I told my wife, "This car is going to have heaters in the seat." (You may be thinking, *That's really not necessary.* Wait a minute! Have you ever sat in a car with a woman? Women usually want to be warmer than men.) Well, she didn't think we could do it, but I said, "We are going to get one." Bless God! We got one!

You must keep a positive attitude or your negative attitude will defeat you. A negative attitude will affect your faith. It will prevent you from succeeding. It will prevent you from receiving wisdom and accomplishing what God has called you to do. We have to be the kind of people who say, "I am going to stay positive about my wife, my kids, my church, and my faith."

We can't win if we allow a negative attitude to envelop us because we close our ears. We won't hear the things that we need to hear and we won't succeed at the level where we need to be.

We can't win if we allow a negative attitude to envelop us because we close our ears. We won't hear the things that we need to hear and we won't succeed at the level where we need to be.

Improving Communication

In marriage, friction and bad attitudes arise because a man doesn't understand the way a woman thinks and a woman doesn't understand the way a man thinks. Communication breaks down all the time.

Here is some information that will help improve your communication, as well as your attitude.

First, let's look at the issue of anger again, and how it affects good communication. Some of the biggest fights within a family are because of lousy communication. Husband, has your wife ever accused you of not listening? Men seem to have a reputation for that.

James 1:19-20 says:

> *So then, my beloved brethren, let every man be swift to hear, slow to speak, slow to wrath; For the wrath of man does not produce the righteousness of God.*

Where does the conflict come in with a man and a woman? Usually it comes to the man who sits down with his remote and watches the game. The wife comes home with a load of groceries. After she puts them away, she sits down and starts to communicate. The man is focused on the game and she is rambling. So typically he says, "Oh, yeah, yeah. That's good, Hon." He doesn't understand (or hear) a word she is saying and he has been able to get by in the past with this kind of response. (I know because I've tried it. My wife started quizzing me one time and that was the end of that little game. She would ask, "Exactly what did I say?" Brain lock!) That's where the friction comes in.

The reason why a husband doesn't listen to his wife sometimes is because he isn't really interested in what she is saying. The woman enjoys the process of communication, but the guy is more interested in getting to the point. She says, "Oh, Honey, we went shopping today. It was so neat. Lois had a different dress on than she had last weekend. I broke one of my nails. You wouldn't believe how my nylons ran." When women get into this process, men are thinking, *Just get to the point!*

When we first married I wasn't as wise as I am now! I would tell my wife, "Get to the point." From the facial expression (and from ducking) I was smart enough to figure out that was not the right approach! But that is why there is a difficulty in communication in marriage.

When I am communicating with my wife, I will indirectly lead her to the point. I am a shepherd. I know what I am doing. She will start to go off on a tangent and I will just pull her back and say, "Oh, now what about that?" and bring her back to the point. If you can keep her on track, she will come to the point faster.

When you speak to each other, use body language.

Here is the conflict: The woman likes the process (the details) and the man likes to bring it to a point (main facts). If we can understand that about each other, communication will improve. If the woman will direct herself more to the point, the husband won't become bored. If you ramble too much, he will start losing the point and start looking at the game.

Here's another tip for good communication.

When you speak to each other, use body language.

Women react to body language. Some guys are so practical they just sit there. The wife asks, "Do you love me?" "Yeah." Men, you need to grab her hand, come up alongside her cheek, and say, "I love you, sweetie." Or, just grab her off her feet. If you're strong enough, pick her up! She will remember that moment for a long time. (And the next day when you are at the chiropractor—you will remember it too!)

Body language is really important. Don't just throw out some words. Have some expression and joy.

Good communication expresses what we are thinking, and it isn't just some words. We really have to add some heart to it. Women like that. So hold her hand and say, "Honey, I want to tell you I love you. You are a tremendous blessing to me." Or when you come home, grab her first thing.

Some men don't do this because they weren't trained that way. It's not my fault you were trained wrong. It's not your wife's fault that you were trained wrong. Just change it. It takes about forty days to change a habit. Why not make a change that will last and that will improve your marriage? Be proactive and DO something about it!

Being Positive with Your Children

"And you, fathers, do not provoke your children to wrath, but bring them up in the training and admonition of the Lord" (Ephesians 6:4).

"Training" is different than "teaching." Training is a hands-on demonstration showing how to do something. The word "fathers" could be translated "parents." It can be either the mother or the father.

A "time-released belief" is a belief learned from the past, and under the right circumstances you will act in response to what you have believed in the past, whether it is right or wrong. An example of this is what happens after you get married and have your first child.

You start raising that first child just the way your father raised you, or the way your mother raised you. That's cool if they raised you according to the Word. But if they didn't, there could be difficulties and problems.

Some parents try to manipulate their children. Manipulation is trying to get someone to do something against their will. They do it against their will simply because they don't want to deal with the negative spirit that comes from the person they are trying to please. Raising children where fear is the motivation will cause them to rebel, and this is why many teenagers go into the "rebellious years."

Favoritism is another rebellion-producing classic in the process of raising children. The child who is not favored will soon become angry and rebellious if favoritism prevails.

It is a good idea to ask yourself, "Did my parents raise me right? Or, is there some room for improvement in the way they raised me?" Why? Because you will most likely train your kids the same way your parents trained you, whether it's right or wrong.

Review the way you are raising your children. Are you doing it according to the Word? Ask yourself, *Is this what the Word says? The Word says I am to spank my child (Proverbs 13:24). My dad never spanked me?* Who are you going to follow, your dad or the Word?

You can go with Dr. Spock and have rebellious kids, or you can go with Jesus. The truth of the matter is that some children need to be spanked, not in anger, but with discipline. Again, every child is different, but you have to make a decision—*I am going to raise my kids the way the Lord says to raise them. "Train up a child in the way he should go, and when he is old, he will not depart from it"* (Proverbs 22:6).

Favoritism is another rebellion-producing classic in the process of raising children. The child who is not favored will soon become angry and rebellious if favoritism prevails.

All of us have made mistakes so I encourage you to change the old belief systems. It is a pro-active world...just do it!

To make a change, evaluate your time-released beliefs and make sure they are according to the Word of God. You will be blessed abundantly above all that you can ask, think, or imagine, once you do this. If you have a positive attitude in obeying God, the best that this world has will become available to you.

"The Best" Is Available to You Now!

Many of us believe that we have to be *of* the world to get the best the world has to offer. That's not true. A lot of good things in this world are *not wrong*, and God says all of those things are within your grasp "if you keep a positive attitude in whatever I have asked you in My Word to do." A positive attitude about forgiveness, about serving, about building projects, about whatever He has led you to do.

Some people give financial offerings but have a bad attitude about it. Likewise, there are people who show up at leadership meetings but don't want to be there. They sit around and hang on to a bad attitude about it, and it affects everyone there. Obviously they have never gotten a hold of this verse in the Word: (Isaiah 1:19) *"If you are willing and obedient, you shall eat the good of the land."* Remember the word "willing" means to breathe after, to be excited about, to consent to something. It means to have a positive attitude in obedience toward God...AND if we have a positive attitude in our obedience, we will eat the good of the land. In other words, we will have the "best" that is available in our culture. God says you can have it "if you keep a positive attitude in your obedience toward Me."

Some ministers have a bad attitude toward the very ministry they were called to. They focus their conversations about all the bad and difficult things that are going on. They don't talk about the good. If you keep talking negatively, you will find yourself on the road to the valley of defeat! You need to stay positive!

Be an "Increase Thinker"

Usually "increase thinkers" have a more positive attitude than most. An increase thinker is a person who expects an increase in everything they do in life. And the Lord is mindful of us when we join with Him in this kind of thinking.

We could apply this to church. God pours His anointing upon the five-fold ministry: apostle, prophet, evangelist, pastor, and teacher. Then, that anointing transcends from the five-fold ministries onto the people, the members within the church, and then out to the world. The church is the core—the place God pours the blessing out. Then it just comes down, like it did upon Aaron when they anointed him with oil. It went down past his beard onto his robe. The blessing of God always hits the church first, then it goes into the people and out into the world.

Psalm 115:13-15 says:

> *He will bless those who fear the Lord, both small and great. May the Lord give you increase more and more, you and your children. May you be blessed by the Lord, who made heaven and earth.*

These verses tell us that increase is cool. As an increase thinker, you won't think in terms of lack. You will think in terms of *increase.*

Let me give you an example. Many people say, "The more money you make, the more money you spend." That is not an increase thinker's way of thinking. An increase thinker, says something like, "The more money I make, the quicker I can get out of debt. The quicker I can get out of debt, the more money I will have. The more money I have, the more money I can give."

"The more money I make, the quicker I can get out of debt. The quicker I can get out of debt, the more money I will have. The more money I have, the more money I can give."

See the difference?

In their minds some people work toward lack instead of increase. You see these people in the church all the time. They are critical and judgmental. When they face a problem all they see is what is wrong. It is the difference between recognizing a glass that is half full or one that is half empty.

When all you see is what is wrong you will miss what is right; and what is right is what you need in order to solve the problem. When you have a positive attitude about a problem, you will be looking for the things that are right within that problem, and you will be attracted to the solution to that problem.

When you are negative, you attract problems.

People with positive attitudes are people who can solve problems. If you have a positive attitude about your problem you will find a solution.

We live in a negative world and the negativity is wrecking our relationships. It is destroying the way we raise our kids, the way we look at life.

Negativity wrecks job opportunities, and when all a disgruntled employee talks about is what is wrong with the company, he or she does more damage than good. A grumbling and complaining employee can shoot himself in the foot, inviting a layoff and a financial need.

When you are negative, you attract problems.

Here's an example of how you can attract problems. If you are having marriage problems and start getting negative about your spouse around your friends, all you will talk about is what is wrong with him or her. All of a sudden you will be attracted to others who are disgruntled with their spouses. As a result, you will pull away from the answers that you need and from the positive people who could help your relationship.

I don't care how difficult or wrong you think your spouse is, don't talk negatively about them in front of anyone. Just go to the Lord, and say, "My husband (or wife) has this or that problem, Lord, but I am believing right now I am not going to dishonor him/her when I am in the presence of other people." "I am not going to dishonor my husband by saying anything about him. I don't care how stinky his feet are." Be careful…don't you dare say anything negative about him in front of other people because there is a woman out there who will take him, stinky feet and all!

So take a stand! Confess positively: "No, I am not going to talk about my mate in a negative way. God put us together, and we are one flesh. I am going to fight for my marriage. I am going to fight for my kids. I am going to fight for my success. I am not going to give in. I am going to fight the good fight of faith and I am going to win. I am going to put the devil under my feet. I am going to step into the blessing and the glory that God has called me to."

When I first started in ministry, we were in the valley a lot. What made the difference was whether or not I could get positive in the middle of the valley. You can make it to the mountaintop by simply being positive. Every person goes through tough situations, but those who stay positive in tough times are the ones God is going to bring out. Praise God!

Chapter Seven

Adjusting Your Attitude

You can't be a positive thinker just because you want to be positive.

You have to actually replace negative thoughts and negative perceptions with positive thoughts and positive perceptions. You must *do* something! When you become aware that your attitude is bad, replace the negative thoughts with positive ones. It is a proactive world, and it's up to you to step out and begin the process. Like the old saying, "It's easier to steer a car that is moving than one that is sitting still." When you step out and do this, you will find that positive thinking becomes part of the package. It is the only way to maintain a winning attitude in life.

Now, let me tell you this; it is easier said than done—but you can do it. It's one thing to have a positive attitude when everything is going good, but it's another thing to have one when everything seems to be going bad. Many times we have to adjust our attitude so our faith will work effectively. That is what we will focus on in this chapter.

Attitude—The Power of the Tongue

As I briefly mentioned in chapter 6, the word "attitude" actually comes from the word "aptitude," which is the inherent talent and ability that every person has to some measure. I believe that a winning attitude actually enhances the gifts and talents that God has given you. This "attitude" will be an integral part of succeeding in every area of your life.

For our faith to work effectively, we must keep a winning attitude in spite of financial challenges, marriage difficulties, or other highly volatile issues.

Many people don't have a clue that life and death are in the power of their tongue!

I believe that what you say with your mouth will affect every aspect of your life (*"Death and life are in the power of the tongue…"* Proverbs 18:21). It has to do with spiritual death, it has to do with sickness and disease in the body, and it even has to do with famine and poverty.

Your words have power. On the positive side, I believe that your words produce every form of life, whether financial success, spiritual success, mental success, or physical success.

Many people don't have a clue that life and death are in the power of their tongue!

They believe something like, "If I watch what I say, I can have more friends, or my wife will be happier." However, I am talking about something much deeper than that. Your attitude is critical. If you lose your winning attitude to the circumstances, you will begin to say negative things that will produce death in your life.

Let me give you an example. If you are having marriage problems and it seems like everything is going from bad to worse to terrible, you no doubt have a bad attitude about it. In the wake of that attitude you may say something like, "We never should have gotten married." If you actually say that (vocalize it) and believe it, you will begin to produce death in the relationship, and there is little chance of it surviving.

Notice what Philippians 4:8 says:

> *Finally, brethren, whatever things are true, whatever things are noble, whatever things are just, whatever things are pure, whatever things are lovely, whatever things are of good report, if there is any virtue and if there is anything praiseworthy—meditate on these things.*

So focus on things that are of good report; sort through the situation and bring out the positives.

As an illustration: One day a little boy wanted to go play baseball. None of his friends were home so he grabbed his mitt, ball, and bat and went out to the schoolyard alone and proceeded to play baseball by himself.

While he is there he speaks out, "I'm the greatest baseball player there is." He takes the ball, throws it up in the air and swings and misses. He looks at the ball and checks it out. Everything seems to be fine, so he says, "I'm still the greatest baseball player in the world."

He throws the ball back up in the air, swings, and misses again. A little bit more frustrated he checks the bat this time. Everything seems fine so he says, "I'm still the best baseball player in the world."

> **When you are exercising faith in God, a positive attitude will bring the miraculous and the blessings to your life that you want and need.**

He throws the ball up a third time, swings, and misses again. Undaunted by his misses he lays the bat down and says, "Strike three, I'm out. And I'm still the greatest *pitcher* in all the world!" This little boy made an adjustment in his thinking.

Sometimes we fail, but it doesn't mean we should surrender our winning attitude, because eventually that winning attitude will cause us to prevail.

When you are exercising faith in God, a positive attitude will bring the miraculous and the blessings to your life that you want and need.

Your thinking may be so negative that it's going to take a lot of work to make it positive. We can compare it to a glass of water, which represents negative thinking. Let's say I have another container, and in this container I have pearls. Those pearls represent the wisdom of God and they represent the positive renewing of your mind.

Now, when you take one of those little pearls out and drop it into the glass of water, it displaces some water. Although the water is still negative, every time you add a pearl, more and more water is displaced. Through this process, eventually the glass is filled with pearls and very little water remains. That's how the mind is renewed to become a positive thinker. It isn't a one-time thing. It is a process that you have to work on until you "fill the glass completely full" with all those pearls of wisdom that you learn from the Word of God. Then, truly, in every situation your thinking will be positive.

Teamwork

I would encourage you to ask a friend or your spouse to help you develop and maintain a positive attitude. My wife and I have an agreement to help one another with ours. Our spouses are the best people in the world to keep the checks and balances because they are with us the most.

Once you have enlisted a friend or family member to help you with your attitude and what you say, give them the liberty to correct you: "If you hear something out of my mouth that obviously is from a negative spirit, check me right on the spot so I can undo it and replace it with a positive thought." I believe this is key.

In America, the family unit has been attacked heavily and it is broken down. Hollywood knows that. This is one reason there are so many programs that are relationship oriented. It seems like we are inundated with one soap after another that centers on dealing with relationships. And the fruit of all this is the alarming statistic that reveals more divorces than ever before. People wonder why kids seem so fragmented and hard to reach.

We have produced a society of people who do not know how to speak or be friends with each other.

We have produced a society of people who do not know how to speak or be friends with each other.

With so much negativity around us, people seem to get offended easily. We need to become positive thinkers so we can have a positive influence on those around us regardless of their negativity.

We need to develop positive relationships with others. As a team we can win our cities to Christ. As a team, we can win the world to Christ, but we will never do it as individuals. To work as a team we've got to learn how to talk to each other and how to love each other, but you can't do that if you have a negative attitude. You can't talk with people who are closed in their spirit or who have a chip on their shoulder. You can't help them because they don't have an ear to hear.

You can decide right now, "I am going to become a positive thinker so I can have a winning attitude. My words will frame prosperity and blessing and a good home life for me. And I am going to seek out counsel and accountability. I want to be a team player in this life."

Your Faith Will Win!

You cannot have a winning attitude if you don't believe your faith can win. It is impossible to maintain a winning attitude if you don't *believe* that faith in God's Word will give you the victory in every situation. You have to *believe* that your situation can get better. You have to *believe* your health can get better. You have to *believe* that your marriage can get better.

Look at Psalm 27:13. It is key to adjusting your attitude for the better. *"I would have lost heart, unless I had believed that I would see the goodness of the Lord in the land of the living."* As you can see, that is not somewhere in the sweet by and by, it is right now!

What does it mean to "lose heart"? It means that you give up on God's best for your life. You give up on His grace and mercy rescuing you out of your situation. You give up on God restoring your family. You give up on God prospering your business. You give up on God prospering your health. You give up on Him and lie down and let the devil run you over. You develop the attitude, "Whatever will be will be." If you do that…you just GAVE UP!

Don't do it! Never ever abandon the will of God for your life. I don't care how hard it is—don't quit! I don't care how discouraged you are—don't quit! Stay in the fight. You might get knocked down, but get back up! You might be discouraged, but get back up! Don't quit!

Positive Faith Moved My Mountain of Infirmity

I was saved at the age of twenty-four. At the time I was doing body and fender work, and fixing automobiles that had been in accidents was my specialty. During that time I developed a throat condition that I had for several years. My throat was sore all the time. I went to several doctors and was continually on medication. It seemed that nothing could help me.

I drank cases of Tab pop every day to soothe my throat because it hurt so badly. I couldn't talk for more than five minutes at a time, and it was like this for months. Consequently I developed an extremely negative attitude.

Finally, I bought a respirator with a hose attached for fresh air. I could wear it while I was doing bodywork so I didn't have to breathe the dust. I did everything I could possibly do. In fact, I even went to a counselor and said, "Maybe you can help me get into a different profession." He started talking about other professions, but dust was involved with all of them.

I decided, "There is no hope for me. What do I do? I am in trouble." I was allergic to dust.

I was so very frustrated. Then my life changed; I got saved, God called me to preach—and something happened to my attitude. Suddenly I just knew that all things were possible to the one who believes. I knew that if God had called me to preach He would heal my throat. I just knew that! So I stepped out in faith and kept my confession right and just stuck with it.

My attitude about this infirmity was positive and I knew in my heart that God would come through. I thought, *If He is God at all, He will come through because He says that those who believe will not be put to shame.* I stuck to it and I changed, and the Lord touched me and healed me.

Whatever your problem is, you have to believe that God can fix it. No matter how big the problem is, you have to believe that He can fix it. So don't quit! Stick with it! God can fix whatever needs His touch. No matter how hard it may seem, God can heal you. He can deliver you and bless you. He will bring you through—so don't ever quit!

Devastation from a Bad Attitude

If you are in a negative situation I want to wake you up so you can make a change.

Let me show you from Scripture the devastation that can happen when you allow a bad attitude to take root in your life. Proverbs 17:20 says, "*He who has a deceitful heart finds no good* [this means the person whose heart is not right with God], *and he who has a perverse tongue falls into evil.*" In other words, this scripture is telling you that if you look at circumstances in your life and all you see is the negative, your heart is not right with God. Don't get mad at me! I didn't write it!

When you have a bad attitude and it sticks with you for any length of time, it not only destroys you, it destroys those you come in contact with. It destroys the people you love. It destroys the people you care about. It destroys the people that you want to love you. When you maintain a bad attitude, you need to adjust it or fix it. If it means asking someone to forgive you, go for it. Whatever you have to do—adjust your attitude! It is the ONE thing that you can change every day of your life…no matter where you are or what you are doing!

This kind of communication can rob a positive-thinking person of his love for the church and for the people in the church, but it can literally destroy the person who has a bad attitude. (Just another reason to do frequent attitude checks.)

My wife Joyce and I have pastored our church for twenty years. During this time we have seen entire families become saved in this ministry. We've seen them saved, healed, and prospering. Many families and individuals love this church because their socks have been blessed off here through the fellowship, support, prayers and ministry while attending. Yet, I have seen friends of these people with negative attitudes influencing them in a negative way and as a result, they lost perspective.

A typical scenario would go like this. During a church service they say, "Wasn't the presence of God good? Wasn't it neat to see all those people saved?" They are rejoicing and talking about it, and suddenly their friend says, "I think the music was too loud." Or, "I wish the pastor would quit preaching on that positive stuff and really get into reality." Or, "I couldn't hear the choir. They weren't loud enough."

This kind of communication can rob a positive-thinking person of his love for the church and for the people in the church, but it can literally destroy the person who has a bad attitude. (Just another reason to do frequent attitude checks.)

I have seen it again and again. There are some things you can't live without, and one is a home church. You cannot live without a sister and a brother in the Body of Christ to love you and care for you. You cannot be spiritually healthy without these relationships. You need to really get this: You need the local church!

My wife has said, "Because of all of the negativity within churches, I know why people sometimes don't go to church." Here's what can happen. You may want to love the people in your church but when someone gets a negative attitude, that negative spirit is deposited in you, and your love for the people that you care so much for can begin to diminish. If you don't stop the effect of that negative spirit, you can begin to fall out of love with these people.

I see the same thing in marriages where a couple is unhappy and they are having problems. The wife has a girlfriend who is in a bad marriage. Her bad attitude about marriage causes some bad seed to be sown. Suddenly that young man she fell in love with is no longer attractive to her, and she is convinced that she no longer loves him. Yet when she first met him, he was all she talked about. She was totally consumed with him. And now they have hit some bumps in the road and she is complaining.

Yet listening to that negative spirit can easily cause both of these ladies to fall out of love with their mates. It is contagious, and divorce is an expensive price to pay over someone having a bad attitude.

It would be safe to say that most Christians believe in marriage and don't plan to divorce. However, some don't like to be around their mates because their mates are negative. They spend as much time as they can away from him or her because of a consistently bad attitude—and they don't want to deal with it.

Don't Drag the Past into the Present

You need to have a winning attitude about your spouse and your children, about your job, and about your church. Many spouses who have been offended in the past keep dragging the offense into the present. When a person becomes offended and they choose not to let go of something that upset them in the past, he or she is spoiling everything that is happening in the present.

Not long ago a lady came to me and asked, "You remember me?" I told her that I was sorry that I did not. She then went on to say, "Well, I was here about fifteen years ago or so." I nodded and asked her how she was doing. And she surprised me when she asked, "Is everyone still talking (negatively) about me?" I couldn't believe it. This lady was still harboring resentment about something that happened years ago that I couldn't even recall. I felt sorry for her because she brought that unhappiness into the present. Life is too short to drag past unhappiness into the present.

When you are with your mate, be happy. Don't drag the negatives that may have happened in the middle of the day into your time together. Let it go. Just say, "Lord, I forgive them. It doesn't matter who is right or wrong. I'm not going to have it in my heart. I forgive them and let the past be past."

Paul said, *"Forgetting those things which are behind and reaching forward to those things which are ahead"* (Philippians 3:13). What lies ahead for you? Prosperity. Happiness. Joy. A mate who knows you better than you know yourself. Children who respect and love you. Having an opportunity to do things you have never done before. That's what lies ahead if you are using your words right.

Adjust your attitude. I don't always have a winning attitude. I get upset, but I have learned that I can't stay in that state very long. I have to fix it quickly, even if it means calling up ten people and apologizing. I will do it because I have to adjust it quickly for my faith to win. You can't put it off until next month. Deal with it right now or you are going to have problems. Don't be a joy killer, but be a person who brings happiness and victory into the lives of others.

Eliminate Those "Little Foxes"

The Song of Solomon 2:15 says, *"Catch us the foxes, the little foxes that spoil the vines, for our vines have tender grapes."* The little foxes represent the little things in your life that can affect your relationship with your mate. The vineyard represents your relationship with each other. Many of you develop a bad attitude toward each other because you don't work on some of the little things that are affecting your relationship. The problem just continues and you don't adjust your attitude, so it becomes fixed.

Why is it that couples don't fix the little things? When the wife says, "Honey, would you please pick up after yourself?" why doesn't it happen? Sometimes it does, but as a rule it doesn't. Or the husband says, "Honey, would you do me a favor and don't hide my keys? Wherever I leave them, just leave them there."

Why is it that many things never get fixed or adjusted? I'll tell you why. Because the wife doesn't think that what the husband wants her to change is that big a deal, so she pacifies him. Likewise, the husband doesn't think that the area his wife wants him to change is any big deal so he pacifies her. So nothing ever gets changed.

Now, if you are sweet to your wife all the time you can get away with some things. (Let that be a word to the wise.) If you take her out to lunch, send flowers, and are considerate of her, all these acts of *going the extra mile* go a long way in your favor.

If a husband determines, "I am going to stay in the good graces of my wife, I am going to work continually on our relationship," she will put up with a lot if she knows you are working on the relationship.

Generally, if I am not under a lot of stress, I am sweet to my wife, but when you get me under pressure like in the middle of a building project, things are likely to be different. You can ask my wife. During a recent building project I wasn't exactly the most sensitive, considerate person in the world. The little things I had stored up along the way made a difference. Our relationship took hits but not ones that could do permanent damage.

I'll give you an example that will reveal one of my imperfections. Recently I had been studying all morning and part of the afternoon for a message and it wasn't coming together right.

I had been on the phone dealing with some issues and my wife brought me lunch.

She said, "Let's go out for dinner tonight and do something different." She started going through a list of all these different restaurants, asking me several questions. I said, "Listen, I can't deal with this right now. I don't have time to deal with this." I was a little sharp.

I said, "My sermon isn't coming together right. Let's just go out to the same old place and do the same old thing because I don't want to deal with it right now."

She went back to the office to work. However, she knew that I wanted to go someplace new but I didn't have the time to plan because I was too distracted and frustrated. She took charge and opened up the entertainment book, pointed her finger and said, "That's where we are going." She made the reservations and I loved her for it.

The place she chose was downtown Seattle and the food wasn't all that good. We were twenty-three stories up where you would expect a great view but the only view was of the next building. All I could say was, "Honey, at least it's something different." And I was still grateful for her efforts in my heart but I didn't show it much outside.

The place had really gotten under my skin. After we ate we returned to our car in the parking garage. All I wanted to do was get out of there. I jumped in and hit the unlock button and looked up to see Joyce standing outside the car. I looked over at her and pointed to the door lock, "It's up! It's up! It's unlocked! Jump in the car!" Very reluctantly she got in the car and I knew something was wrong. She looked over at me and said, "I hesitated in getting in because I wanted to give you an opportunity to open the door for me."

I felt so bad. In a flash of "repentance" I ran around to her side of the car and opened the door. I couldn't get her to get back out because she was too embarrassed. Another lesson learned and I just shut the door and climbed back in.

Be Quick to Adjust

Quick adjustments in situations like this are critical. I made mine and let me tell you about it.

When we got home I had my chance. Our garage opens with a door opener and normally when we drive in she jumps out of the car and goes in the house just like I do. This time as soon as I parked the car, I said, "Don't move. Don't you dare get out of the car." I jumped out of the car, walked around to her door, opened it, and said, "You can come out now, my queen." Then, I gave her a kiss.

> Be sensitive to your mate's "pressure."

A woman will love you if you make an effort. But ladies have to understand that when the husband is under pressure he may not be as considerate as he would be if he weren't under such pressure.

Here is a truth that I want you to see. This will show you the importance of not letting a negative attitude be carried on in your life.

Be Sensitive to Your Mate's "Pressure"

Suppose a husband is under great pressure on his job and he comes home frustrated. The boss is asking too much. He sits down and tries to chill out by watching a game. He has had pressure all day and just wants to relax.

The wife has been working all day and she swings by the grocery store, picks up a trunk load of groceries, and comes home. She gets out of the car, comes in with one bag of groceries, and sees her husband sitting on the couch.

They greet one another, but she has an expectation that he doesn't have a clue about. She sets the sack down and wants (expects) him to get up and go out and get the rest of the groceries. She doesn't want to have to tell him. She wants him to do it on his own—without being told. He is lost in the game and relaxing and doesn't respond.

The wife goes out and gets every bag. With each one she gets, the angrier she becomes. This goes on and then she begins to make noises in the kitchen and drops a few things. She thinks that might get his attention but he's totally out of it.

He asks, "Are you okay? You didn't break anything, did you?" She continues putting things away and then begins to make a few negative statements. He still doesn't respond and doesn't think anything of what is going in the kitchen.

At dinnertime he doesn't make any comments on the dinner being burnt. That evening after he has watched the movies and chilled out and read his paper he suddenly gets the romantic urge. He looks over at her and she knows what he wants but she has a surprise for him. She has a negative attitude just waiting to get revenge. She has had the bad attitude for three or four hours and there is no way he will get anywhere near her—she has made a conclusion and it is summed up with a solid "no!"

Communicate Your Expectations

I always tell my wife, "Honey, I can't read your mind. I do not know what you are thinking. I don't have any idea what your expectations are in this situation. Don't let me fumble through it. Just tell me clearly what you want." And she does. For example, I'm sitting there and she says, "Hey! I need someone to get the groceries out of the car."

> I have learned that success in any field demands that you do some things you don't necessarily want to do.

When we were first married Joyce wanted to make sure I remembered our anniversary so she gave me several reminders. Even today if we're in the mall and she wants something for Christmas or birthday, she says, "Boy, isn't that neat?" She knows I am not getting it, so she says, "This is a hint! A hint! A hint! Buy this for me!"

Many men, especially when under pressure, tend to get focused in on the problem and they don't always see the things that they need to see. But if the woman will communicate her expectations to her husband, after a while he will begin to pick up on things on his own. All things are possible!

Be Willing to Serve

Usually I know what my wife wants me to do because over the years she has conditioned and trained me. I know certain things she expects and things she gets upset about if I don't do. As long as it's a reasonable thing, I go ahead and do it. That's no big deal. I am here to serve her. The thing we are to do in ministry, as well as in marriage, is to serve.

I have learned that success in any field demands that you do some things you don't necessarily want to do.

The key is, you have to have a winning attitude. How do you do things that your wife or your husband wants you to do, but you don't really want to do? First, you have to understand how much it means to him or her.

Here's a case in point. For some reason, my wife likes cruise ships. We have been on two cruises in the last two years and the last one was a seven-day excursion. I like being out on the water, but toward the end of that week, everything was moving!

Joyce and I were watching television together when a commercial came on. Here's a cruise ship and a beach. I said, "Beach, good. Boat, bad." I went through the whole commercial like that. My wife stopped and said, "You need to develop a positive attitude toward cruise ships."

I said, "Honey, I will take you on a cruise ship. Whether I really want to go or not, I will take you on it." She said, "I don't want to go on it unless you really want to go." I knew right then that I needed to develop a positive attitude toward cruise ships!

Focus on the "Good"

How do you develop a positive attitude toward a cruise ship? It's really not that hard. You focus on the good things on the cruise ship until you have focused on so many things that are better than the negative things you know about, your attitude improves.

For many women there is something about being on the water and cruise ships that is a romantic experience. That's a good thing. The other good thing is, you can eat and eat and eat and it's a really good thing...until you have to get off the boat.

One of the reasons I didn't like the seven-day cruise that we were on is because I didn't get to go snorkeling! I could have paid to go on a snorkeling tour, but I didn't. The next time I go on a cruise, that's what I'll do differently—I'll make sure it includes a snorkeling tour. That way, I'll enjoy it more and my attitude will be better. Regardless, I'll take my wife on another one because it means so much to her.

Now, going on a cruise ship won't make your marriage better. What makes your marriage better is when you are willing to do something that you normally don't like to do and get a positive attitude about it simply because it means a lot to your spouse. It doesn't have to be a cruise ship. It could be something else that means a lot to your wife or to your husband. Do something you wouldn't normally do.

The wife may have a totally negative attitude about going to a game with her husband. But if it really means that much to him for you to go, then find out all the good things you can about the game so you can go with a positive attitude. Women...that will speak volumes of how much you love your husband.

Adjust to Please Your Mate

Most men are not asked to go shopping with their wives. Why? Well, because we husbands find it hard to adjust our attitudes when we are shopping! When I am at the mall I can always tell a husband who doesn't want to be there. He is sitting with his head down. The wife is running around frantically trying to make her purchases quickly and he's grumping and growling at her. She finds a chair and says, "Honey, here's a chair where you can wait." All this hassle really steals the joy of shopping for a woman. It's like she has to drag this two-hundred-pound sack of rocks around!

Be willing to do the things you don't want to do, and then do them in a positive way!

We need to learn to adjust our attitudes in the things we don't want to do so we can please the one we love. It is key in showing your love to your spouse and a primary key to success in your marriage.

Be willing to do the things you don't want to do, and then do them in a positive way!

Chapter Eight

Possessing a Winner's Attitude

When you learn how to fly a plane, one of things they teach you is how to "trim" the aircraft. What this means is that the plane is balanced while in flight. When it is trimmed properly, it will go a greater distance with the fuel it has taken on.

In a similar manner if we can learn how to adjust ("trim") our attitude in the storms of life, we will go the distance that God has called us to.

What are you facing? Perhaps it is a divorce and the challenges involved with visitation privileges and having your children going from house to house. Maybe you are confronted with the mistakes of the past, or financial difficulties. Whatever you are up against, I just want to encourage you to trim your attitude, and allow God to balance you out for the long haul.

One of the best ways to have a positive attitude is to have your faith exercised toward God's will. As you begin to pursue His will in your life, you will see the blessings of God begin to manifest in your life. Just bear in mind, to have positive faith and a winning attitude we must work on it constantly.

Cross Bearing

Many people don't understand that the miraculous power of Christ operates through the faith of people. Whenever Jesus found faith, the miraculous happened. I am bringing that out because in Matthew, chapter 8, where Jesus healed the sick, it makes a special note that *all* of the people were healed.

That is very important because the next verse, verse 17, shows us why that happened: "*That it might be fulfilled which was spoken by Isaiah the prophet, saying, 'He Himself took our infirmities and bore our sicknesses.'*" That is a reference taken from Isaiah 53:4-5. Verse 5 reads, "*But He was wounded for our transgressions, He was bruised for our iniquities; the chastisement for our peace was upon Him, and by His stripes we are healed.*" This is a direct reference to Jesus going to the cross and bearing not only sin but sickness as well. This is a special kind of "cross bearing."

If it is God's will for you to be healed, then your faith should be fighting for health. It is your faith that needs to bear the cross!

I believe many people have misunderstood the subject of cross bearing mentioned in the Bible, which speaks of two crosses: 1) The one we are to carry when we follow Christ; and 2) The cross that Christ bore. Let's look at this because sometimes people with life burdens (poverty, illness, etc.) have a tendency to think, *This is my cross to bear for Christ.* I think this is a good time to find out what cross you are to bear and what cross Jesus has already borne for you.

Let's look again at Matthew 8. Verse 16 states, "*When evening had come, they brought to Him many who were demon-possessed. And He cast out the spirits with a word, and healed all who were sick.*" Jesus did not heal everyone in every region where He went, but He was carrying the cross for those He was healing. The healing itself was a sacrifice of atonement, and healing is in the atonement. I don't mean to sound harsh or insensitive to people who are suffering with illness, but I do know that if it is God's will for you to be healed, then your faith should be fighting for health. It is your faith that needs to bear the cross!

If you want to have a positive attitude about life, you have to understand that God is not the one who is putting sickness and disease on you. Sin is what brings sickness and disease. There wasn't any sickness and disease until sin came into the world. Now, that doesn't mean that if you are sick, you are in sin. But somewhere sin has created that sickness and it is God's will for you to be delivered and made whole.

David confirmed this in Psalm 103:1-3:

> *Bless the Lord, O my soul; and all that is within me, bless His holy name!*
>
> *Bless the Lord, O my soul, and forget not all His benefits: Who forgives all your iniquities, who heals all your diseases.*

We have never had a problem believing that God will forgive us of all our sins, but sometimes we do have a problem believing that it is His will to heal us of every infirmity.

I want you to fight for the health that God has provided for you through Christ's victory on the cross. He took your infirmities and bore away your sicknesses. That's why the early Church was so adamant about this.

James was a pastor at the Jerusalem church, the mother Church of all churches, and he said this:

> *Is anyone among you sick? Let him call for the elders of the church, and let them pray over him, anointing him with oil in the name of the Lord.*
>
> *And the prayer of faith will save the sick, and the Lord will raise him up. And if he has committed sins, he will be forgiven (James 5:14-15).*

Later on, during the Dark Ages, unbelief came into the Church about healing people suffering from sickness. The good news is that God has lit up the place now. It is no longer dark!

It is God's will that you be well. It is God's will to rescue you physically as well as to forgive you. But God did more than that on the cross. Jesus bore more than your sin and sickness. He also became a curse that you might receive the blessings of Abraham. If Jesus bore your sins and sicknesses, why should you bear them? If this doesn't give you a positive attitude, there is something wrong with your joystick!

Galatians 3:13-14 says:

> *Christ has redeemed us from the curse of the law* [the curse of the law is basically the curse of failing at whatever you do], *having become a curse for us (for it is written, "Cursed is everyone who hangs on a tree"), That the blessing of Abraham might come upon the Gentiles in Christ Jesus, that we might receive the promise of the Spirit through faith.*

That the blessing of Abraham might come upon the Gentiles in Christ Jesus, that we might receive the promise of the Spirit through faith.

In other words, Jesus became a curse for you on the cross so the blessings of God, which are mostly spiritual and financial, would come upon you. That's what Jesus bore on that cross. Grace, mercy, and provision are in the atonement. As a born-again believer you are a covenant partner with God, and you have incredible benefits!

It takes faith to draw on these provisions. But I'll tell you what, when I was sick all the time and some preacher got up and preached that it was God's will to heal me, I was encouraged and all of a sudden my attitude became positive! I shifted into high gear again and had a winning attitude with the spirit of faith once again operating in me.

You don't know the will of God until you know His Word, and you can't have faith until you know His Word. But once you know His Word, you have His will and you will have enough faith for your miracle. (And be careful never to judge someone else if they are sick. Just pray and stand in faith for them. That is cross bearing.)

God really desires to deliver each of us from anything that we are failing or unsuccessful at. He wants to unblock what is hindering us physically and He wants to help us overcome the areas of sin that hinder us. Just remember and claim that God delivered us from it all through the cross! We are heirs to the Kingdom and we can draw on His provision, *now*!

Jesus said to His followers, "*If anyone desires to come after Me, let him deny himself, and take up his cross, and follow Me*" (Matthew 16:24). What is He talking about? When you come to Christ, whether you like it or not, you have to give up your agenda and take on God's agenda. You have to come to Him on His terms, sort of like when Isaiah said, "Lord, here I am, Your servant. Whatever You want me to do, I will do."

Taking up your cross means to deny yourself. That's part of the way true salvation works. You step out and take up the cross that goes with His calling and purpose for your life. It is obedience and obedience is much better than sacrifice.

Forms of Persecution

One form of persecution is when unbelievers come against you. In 2 Timothy 3:12 Paul said, "*Yes, and all who desire to live godly in Christ Jesus will suffer persecution.*" Another form is when God blesses you so much that those around you get jealous. Remember what Jesus said to His own disciples who had left everything?

> *Assuredly, I say to you, there is no one who has left house or brothers or sisters or father or mother or wife or children or lands, for My sake and the gospel's,*

Who shall not receive a hundredfold now in this time—houses and brothers and sisters and mothers and children and lands, with persecutions—and in the age to come, eternal life" Mark 10:29-30.

The hundredfold is confirmed in the Old Testament. There was a famine in the land, and Isaac was going to go down to Egypt to get supplies. But God spoke to him, giving him directions as to what he was to do:

Then the Lord appeared to him and said: "Do not go down to Egypt; live in the land of which I shall tell you.

"Dwell in this land, and I will be with you and bless you; for to you and your descendants I give all these lands, and I will perform the oath which I swore to Abraham your father..."

Then Isaac sowed in that land, and reaped in the same year a hundredfold; and the Lord blessed him.

The man began to prosper, and continued prospering until he became very prosperous;

For he had possessions of flocks and possessions of herds and a great number of servants. So the Philistines envied him" (Genesis 26:2-3,12-14).

Did you read that? God prospered him so much that the Philistines envied him! God wants to bless the Body of Christ so much that unbelievers will be drawn to the church, saying, "I want to get to know your God. If God can do that for you, I want to get to know Him too." That is a holy envy.

For years the church has been beaten up and (financially) broke and this doesn't appeal to someone who is looking for assurance and security. In the Old Testament it wasn't like that. Other nations envied Israel. They envied the blessing of God because God made the Israelites the head and not the tail. They were above and not beneath. They would lend and never borrow because they had so much money. I like that! We are talking about a positive faith.

Exercising Mountaintop Faith!

When you know the will of God you can exercise faith. This is something to really get ahold of. If you are in the valley, you can exercise your faith and expect that God will come through. Believe it...God is going to bless you. It's easy to have a positive attitude when you know God's will is working for you.

It was God's will to heal me of my throat condition, and today it is God's will to prosper me. He wants to heal and prosper you too. It is God's will that has come through in my life, and He has not been denied. I'm telling you, when God's blessings are manifest in your life, it produces a positive attitude like you've never seen. This is not the gospel of bad news. It is the gospel of good news!

Regardless of where you are right now, if you have faith in God and keep exercising that faith and applying a positive attitude, God will bring you out of the valley onto the mountaintop. It is His nature and it is His will.

You will go no higher in life than your attitude. You need a positive winning attitude to keep going higher. And if you work to develop a consistently positive attitude, you will excel in everything you do—in your marriage, in raising your kids, in church service, and in leadership. You will soar!

When we hire anyone at our church, the first thing I look for is a positive attitude. We look at the skills secondarily. (You can always teach a person skills. But if a person is a negative thinker, you can get them as skillful as you want and they will sabotage everything by their negative thinking.)

Attitude affects everything we do. One of the things we wrestle with in the church is relationship issues stemming from attitude problems. When these kinds of issues drift over into leadership, it brings a whole new set of problems. If you are unhappy in the home, that unhappiness will be displayed in your leadership style. It will cause you to have a bad attitude toward people that you need to minister to. We cannot win others to Christ unless we can get along with people—and that takes a positive attitude. We must be careful to have a positive attitude check on a regular basis.

Reciprocating One Flesh

Men need women and women need men. It is clear from the very beginning. Let's look at the creation of the woman from the man in Genesis 2:21-24:

> *And the Lord God caused a deep sleep to fall on Adam, and he slept; and He took one of his ribs, and closed up the flesh in its place.*
>
> *Then the rib which the Lord God had taken from man He made into a woman, and He brought her to the man.*
>
> *And Adam said: "This is now bone of my bones and flesh of my flesh; she shall be called Woman, because she was taken out of Man.*
>
> *"Therefore a man shall leave his father and mother and be joined to his wife, and they shall become one flesh.*

Now, what does that mean? When God first created Adam, within Adam were all of the feminine qualities as well as the masculine qualities of mankind. He was made in the likeness and image of God, and he was made to have dominion. But when God caused him to sleep, He took a rib out of Adam's side. As He removed it, He took out the feminine qualities that would form the woman for this reason. *"And they shall become one flesh"* is amplified because now the man is incomplete without the woman, and the woman is incomplete without the man. They need one another.

Every man needs the feminine touch of a woman. Leave it to a man and he would have something like moose heads hanging where something more pleasant or aesthetic could be. But as soon as you get married and a woman comes into your house, she puts her touch on it. Visitors look around and compliment you both on what a pleasant home you have. This really has little to do with the husband, who may have done the work on the house, but it has quite a bit to do with the woman, who artistically put it all together.

Something of interest to those single folks. Even though I am incomplete without my wife and my wife is incomplete without me, let me say this in behalf of the singles.

When you are single, you are complete in Christ. But the moment you get married, forget it. You are incomplete without your mate.

When you are single, *you are complete in Christ.* But the moment you get married, forget it. You are incomplete without your mate.

Positive Attitude and Patience Go Together

I go shopping with my wife and wait for her someplace in the mall while she goes off and shops. One of the things that she is notorious for is not coming back at the appointed time. She justifies it by saying, "You only gave me twenty minutes to get to the other end of the mall." I am waiting for an additional half hour, sometimes an hour, for her to meet me at the designated spot. I have learned to handle it and I have gained patience with it over the years. I am now able to keep a positive attitude toward her. Even though it is something that still irritates me, how do I stay positive about it?

Well, now when I go shopping with her I always say, "I will meet you here at 3:00." I know that means 4:00. I plan alternate things to do like play video games. She knows if she is gone too long it will be a very expensive afternoon. I want you to hear this. Her tardiness might appear to be a weakness but actually it comes from her strength.

I've noticed that many men can be on time because we are pretty much goal oriented and focused on what we go after. However, women are usually multi-task oriented and seem to always have ten to thirty things going on in their minds (which is a sure sign of high intelligence, praise the Lord!). Well, because of this ability, she is buying birthday presents, anniversary presents, Christmas presents, baby shower presents before there is a baby shower, all sorts of presents! So she is gifted in that area because she wants to make sure that her nest—her home and family—is taken care of. It's a gift but the gift causes her to be tardy!

In the case of me and my wife, I can now be patient with her and have a positive attitude toward her because of the adjustment in thinking I have made over the years. A good way to think about it is to simply adjust my thinking to thoughts like, "she is shopping primarily for me or our family." Or "That's just the way women are." I can accept it because it's her gift.

One of my downfalls is that I have a tendency to be single-minded about things. I focus in on one thing and I can't seem to get focused on anything else at the same time. My mind gets completely consumed with one thing.

This is troubling to my wife, especially when she may want to have a discussion about something. Here I am focusing in on some mountain-moving problem, looking for a solution. As I am consumed with finding an answer, she breaks my train of thought and wants my opinion about what color the walls should be painted. At the moment I don't care about the color of the walls, and tell her so. I know she gets irritated, but she is patient with me and remains positive when she could very well lose it instead.

Sometimes she will just stop and hold my face and say, "Honey, snap to. Here I am." She will look at me and say, "Wake up! Come on, focus." She does that when I am driving too because often when I drive I am still working on the problem in my mind. I'm doing that and all of a sudden we are in a nearby town and I didn't intend to go there! Joyce merely says, "Honey, turn the car around." and she understands. She has been around me long enough to know that I am functioning in the gift of problem solving.

We must have a positive attitude toward each other. We can't shrink back from it. I learned a long time ago that my wife doesn't always mean what she says or say what she means. I have to interpret it. But once you understand how she functions, you can have a positive attitude, because you realize she is uniquely made and she is a blessing.

Christ Loves the Church

Jesus prayed that the Church would be unified. Today, there is more of a unified effort in the Body of Christ to do something for the Kingdom of God than in all of previous Church history.

However, we still need tremendous people skills and effort to keep a positive attitude toward one another to maintain unity, even toward those who have failed or dropped the ball. Do not allow yourself to have a bad attitude, for once you do, you won't be patient with other people.

If you're not patient with others, you can't help them.

If you're not patient with others, you can't help them.

This positive attitude in the affairs of the Church or in dealing with the things of God is transferred into your job. If you get a bad attitude toward your supervisors, you will not be able to learn from them. They will pick up on it and you could be the first one on the list to go should downsizing occur. You have to develop a positive attitude and maintain it.

Many people don't think they have a bad attitude. Yet a spirit of complacency is a negative attitude, and many Christians succumb to this. They are not aggressive or motivated on their job—or for the work of the ministry. They make little or no effort to reach their neighbors for Christ. They show up for church but beyond that do nothing to reach out. We must change that. We need a positive spirit about what God is doing in our lives. We can't let the neighborhood go to hell. We can reach our neighborhoods.

Even if you think those around you aren't receptive—you can make a positive difference in their lives. I have tried to find a man I worked with in body-and-fender work years ago. He was a painter and he was always preaching to me. I did everything but hit him. I mean, I cursed him. I told him what I thought of him. I was mean to him. I persecuted him. As far as I know he doesn't even know I am saved and now preaching the gospel.

Even though I mistreated this man for years, I remember the time when one of my freshwater fish died and it was this man who gave me a fish to replace it. I was an unbeliever at the time and it made a lasting impression on me.

An Enthusiastic Attitude of Obedience

Have you been griping and complaining on your job or about your job? Not getting that promotion or getting ahead? Well, God's eyes are looking to and fro throughout the earth and He is looking for enthusiastic obedience. He could be passing you over because "the good of the land" (Isaiah 1:19) only goes to the person who obeys with a *positive attitude!*

Perhaps you have been tithing and giving and doing everything you can think of to be right with God. And still you are getting passed over for promotion, and missing other blessings that you may be expecting

The problem may be your attitude. You may be throwing your check in the offering with a negative attitude, saying, "Take it, Lord!" Or, you may be serving in the church and asking, "Do I have to go again? I don't want to go today. I want to stay home and watch the game."

Isaiah 1:19 says, *"If you are willing and obedient, you shall eat the good of the land."* The word "willing" refers to someone with a positive attitude who is energetic and has an enthusiastic attitude of obedience. We could read this verse like this: *If you have a winning attitude and are enthusiastic in your obedience, you shall eat the good of the land.* The "good of the land" refers to the best that you can get from the world that is good. The best! But you won't get it without a positive attitude.

God wants to bless you with the best, but your obedience must be accompanied by a positive attitude. You have to adjust your attitude and then maybe readjust it over and over again. That is working with God rather than against Him, and He will give you the good of the land to eat.

Thoughts Are Like Magnets

When you have a negative attitude, expect bad things to happen. Your negative thoughts attract those bad things.

How many times have you thought, "What else could go wrong today?" Are you expecting to get laid off? How about getting into a fight with your boss? Or stuck in traffic? Or worse...how about an accident in that traffic? Your thoughts are like magnets. If you have positive thoughts you will attract positive things. But if you have negative thoughts, you will attract negative things.

An adulterous man attracts adulterous women. There is a spiritual force going on that we cannot see, and it is affected by our faith. We are spiritual beings, and because of that, our attitude affects the output of our faith.

When my attitude is bad and my faith is negative, that's exactly what it attracts. It attracts conflict and unhappiness. At the same time God is saying, "Adjust your thinking so your attitude will be positive. Change your perspective and believe Me once again. If you do, My blessings will flow to you."

Your expectancy affects everything in your life. If your attitude is negative, you will not succeed at the level God has called you to. Be positive. If you get a pink slip on your job, you can be positive. Look at it as an opportunity to pursue something new and better. Look at your mountains as stepping-stones. Be proactive and make a decision to think differently about difficulties you face. When you do, you will release your faith.

Winners Are Positive Thinkers

After you have prayed in faith about the challenge or difficulty you are facing (and after you quit worrying), the final thing you need to do is described in Philippians 4:8:

> *Finally, brethren, whatever things are true, whatever things are noble, whatever things are just, whatever things are pure, whatever things are lovely, whatever things are of good report, if there is any virtue and if there is anything praiseworthy—meditate on these things.*

A Winner Thinks in Terms of "Addition" and "Multiplication"

Maybe you need to get an examination from the neck up! You may be facing regrets confronting mistakes you made in the past. Here is a simple key that will help you to be a positive thinker rather than a negative thinker: *Positive thinkers think in terms of addition and multiplication. Negative thinkers think in terms of subtraction. They think in ways that subtract from the good in things.*

Let's say a man takes his wife out for their anniversary. They are at a nice restaurant having a good time and the wife asks how he likes his meal. He replies, "The meat isn't cooked well enough." He is a negative thinker and he speaks in terms of subtraction. A positive thinker multiplies the good in a situation. He could have said, "It is fine but I may have the cook warm up the meat a little. By the way, how is yours? Can I have him warm yours a bit too?" It's a choice to be a positive thinker or a negative thinker. Examine the way you think about the conflicts and difficulties you face.

A positive thinker creates an abundance mentality, which is: *there is more than enough. I have no lack.* On the other hand, a negative thinker thinks in terms of lack and what he or she can't get.

Negativity Isolates You from Wisdom

Negative thinking will cause you to isolate yourself from wise people, while positive thinking will cause you to associate with people who have wisdom.

If you stay in the negative mode very long, you will begin to draw isolated kinds of conclusions. "The only person who is ever blessed is the one who takes advantage of poor people." "Everyone in this business has wealth. They stole it or did something illegal to get it." With that kind of negative thinking, you isolate yourself from the wisdom that can take you to the top.

I see people who allow negative thinking to isolate them from church. Even though they call themselves Christians, they won't attend church. They have a negative attitude and fail to realize that the blessing they need from God comes through the church. Often they are thinking negative of some bad experience of the past and as a result, they believe people in the church are hypocrites or flakey. The truth is, they themselves are hypocrites for not being in church because they are not practicing the Word.

Surrendered and Unified

How can you be a Christian and not be involved with the work of the ministry? The whole purpose of getting saved and being here on Earth is to win people to Christ. Otherwise, when you were saved God should have taken you to heaven immediately! He has left you here to do His bidding. He wants us to identify with our fellow humans and share the Good News. And, just remember, Jesus is not coming back until the Church gets together and does the work of the ministry.

If one generation would globally evangelize the world, Jesus would come back and get this whole thing over. He would usher in the millennium and we would be happy campers! But the Church must unify for the purpose of leading people to Christ.

Amos 9:13 says:

> *Behold, the days are coming," says the Lord, "when the plowman shall overtake the reaper, and the treader of grapes him who sows seed; the mountains shall drip with sweet wine, and all the hills shall flow with it.*

Verses 11 and 12 put this in context:

> *On that day I will raise up the tabernacle of David* [a reigning tabernacle], *which has fallen down, and repair its damages; I will raise up its ruins, and rebuild it as in the days of old;*
>
> *"That they may possess the remnant of Edom, and all the Gentiles who are called by My name," says the Lord who does this thing.*

What a promise! However, this is not going to happen until we unite and have a winning attitude. I mean, every one of us must have a winning attitude. We must approach the problems we face with a positive spirit of faith to receive the level of blessing God wants to pour upon our lives.

If you study the Bible you will find that a few extremely fruitful men mastered this. The Apostle Paul is a classic example of one who mastered it. Remember when he and Silas were beaten with rods and thrown into the inner jail? If being treated like this doesn't give you a bad attitude, I don't know what will. I mean, they are hurting and what do they do? They start singing praises to God. That positive spirit caused God to release His power, which brought an earthquake, shook their chains loose, and provided a setup for the jailer and his household to be saved. That's what a positive attitude will do! Their release from jail was not only a release but the means for an entire family to be saved. That is addition and multiplication!

Count It All Joy!

No matter how down he was, Paul had the ability to count everything joy. He rejoiced always. His entire letter to the Philippians was about rejoicing. In chapter 4, verse 4, Paul said, *"Rejoice in the Lord always. Again I will say, rejoice!"*

This incredible human being was chained up in Caesar's palace with a Praetorian guard watching him when he wrote that. He was in shackles, yet he was free. Paul indicated that his imprisonment was for the furtherance of the gospel. Why? Because when he was chained to the Praetorian guards, who were responsible for putting the rulers into office, he was able to preach to them. He was not chained to them—they were chained to him! Now that is a positive thinker.

People came to see Paul where he was imprisoned and he would preach to them. It had to be one of the first "jail ministries."

The power of God is incredible. Paul took a negative situation and made it into a positive one. That's why he bore more fruit than all of the other apostles. He knew the power of prayer and thanksgiving. He wrote, *"Be anxious for nothing, but in everything by prayer and supplication, with thanksgiving, let your requests be made known to God"* (Philippians 4:6).

In your life, if you are working for a difficult person, you may have to go off by yourself from time to time and say, "Lord, I give thanks *in* all things. I rejoice because I am a light in a dark place." Then, God will use your positive spirit.

We need to be as persevering as the mule I heard about in a story. It goes something like this. There was a farmer who had a mule. One day as the mule was backing up, he fell into a dry well. The farmer, wanting to get him out, tried to put a rope around him to pull him out but he couldn't do it. Finally, he came to the conclusion, "I can't get this mule out." Since he thought the mule was going to die, he said, "I will back my dump truck up and fill the hole with dirt."

Dirt started going into the hole, but suddenly the farmer heard a snorting sound. The mule kept climbing up on top of the dirt. As the man kept pouring dirt in, the mule kept climbing. Finally, the mule reached the top and jumped out. He was determined that he wouldn't stay in that hole and die.

Faith is released when you have a winning attitude. It's easy to be positive when everything is going well. But it's the ability to adjust in all seasons that determines your greatness!

Maybe you have been in a dry hole too long. You have been in a negative spirit too long. You need to climb up out of it and give God praise and thanksgiving. Climb up out and say, "Lord, I am not going to have a bad attitude. Regardless of how far down I am right now, I am going to climb out with a positive attitude."

Faith is released when you have a winning attitude. It's easy to be positive when everything is going well. But it's the ability to adjust *in all seasons* that determines your greatness!

If anyone can be positive in this negative world it should be people in the church since God has "*given to us all things that pertain to life and godliness…*" (2 Peter 1:3).

When people see that you can go through the same kind of problems they are going through, but you remain positive, you display a strength that will attract them to you and your lifestyle. Your positive approach to life, through the gospel, will cause them to want the Jesus Christ in you. They will also want Him as their Lord, Savior, and Friend! They too will become winners by the way they think. Perhaps the only Jesus they will ever see is the Jesus that exudes from you and your attitude. And you and I both know that Jesus Christ will cause their faith to soar—and they will grow positive in this negative world!

About the Author

Jack Holt is Senior Pastor of River of Life Fellowship, a vibrant and rapidly growing non-denominational church located in Kent, Washington. Pastor Jack is a dynamic teacher, leader and spiritual mentor. His powerful and motivating messages are filled with life-changing truths from the Word of God that will build your faith and help you live a fulfilled and victorious life.

Growing Positive in a Negative World
Order Form

Postal orders: Jack Holt Ministries
River of Life Fellowship
10615 SE 216th Street
Kent, WA 98031

Telephone orders: 253-859-0832

E-mail orders: info@riveroflifefellowship.org
Website bookstore: www.riveroflifefellowship.org

Please send *Growing Positive in a Negative World* to:

Name: ______________________________

Address: ______________________________

City: __________________ State: ________ Zip: __________

Telephone: (_____) ______________

Book Price: $11.99

Shipping: $3.00 for the first book and $1.00 for each additional book to cover shipping and handling within US, Canada, and Mexico. International orders add $6.00 for the first book and $2.00 for each additional book.